Books by Ed Gorman

The Sam McCain Series

The Day the Music Died
Wake Up Little Susie

The Jack Dwyer Series

New, Improved Murder • *Murder Straight Up* •
Murder in the Wings • *The Autumn Dead* •
A Cry of Shadows

The Tobin Series

Murder on the Aisle • *Several Deaths Later*

The Robert Payne Series

Blood Moon • *Hawk Moon* • *Harlot's Moon*

Suspense Novels

The Night Remembers • *Night Kills* • *Black River Falls*

Thrillers

The Marilyn Tapes • *The First Lady* • *Runner in the
Dark* • *Senatorial Privilege*

Short-Story Collections

Prisoners • *Cages* • *Dark Whispers* •
Moonchasers • *Famous Blue Raincoat*

Will You Still Love Me Tomorrow?

A Mystery

Ed Gorman

CARROLL & GRAF PUBLISHERS, INC.
NEW YORK

First Carroll & Graf edition 2001

Carroll & Graf Publishers, Inc.
A Division of Avalon Publishing Group
19 West 21st Street
New York, NY 10010-6805

Library of Congress Cataloging-in-Publication Data is available.
ISBN: 0-7867-0775-5

Manufactured in the United States of America

For Kent Carroll, who had the faith

For reliable editorial help, thanks to Ron Adkins,
Michael Barson, and Deb Brod

I smell blood and an era of prominent madmen.

—W. H. Auden

PART I

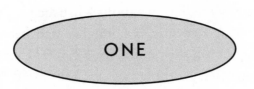

ONE

GEE," THE BEAUTIFUL PAMELA Forrest said. "He actually looks kinda dopey."

And he did.

Here he was, the world's first nuclear-powered bogeyman, and he looked like the uncle everybody feels sorry for because he's fat and sloppy.

Nikita Khrushchev. Premier of the Soviet Union. The world's number-one Russian. Not to mention Communist.

On this warm sunny twenty-first day of September, 1959, "Nikki," as some of the press had taken to calling him, had come to a large Iowa farm as part of his trip to the United States. A farmer-businessman named Roswell Garst had invited him here. Garst had quite the spread.

"And his suit looks so cheap," the beautiful Pamela went on. "And he sweats so much."

I smiled. "Too bad he doesn't look more like Frankie Avalon, huh?"

She smiled back. "Yes. Or Rock Hudson."

Just then there was a small ruckus toward the back of the

crowd. Protesters with signs that read DEATH TO THE COMMIES and BETTER DEAD THAN RED jeered old Nikki. While most Iowans despised communism, they believed in being polite to visitors. And they were curious about Khrushchev and were tired of the Cold War. Recently, a company had been going door-to-door selling bomb shelter kits for $2,500. That was the price of a new Chevrolet. Nothing is more admirable than turning a buck on the terrors of nuclear holocaust. The last ten years, grade school counselors had seen an increasing number of little ones who had nightmares about nuclear war. It was the age of the atom, all right. Just about every commercial you saw on TV had something atomic in it. Atomic-powered cars, refrigerators, toothpaste. Personally, I never went anywhere without my atomic-powered jockey shorts.

The crowd—farmers, businessmen, teachers, school kids— were shouting for the protesters to be quiet. Roswell Garst, the farm's owner and a very wealthy hybrid seed corn pioneer, had set up a press conference in his front yard. Reporters were asking Khrushchev questions about Russian farming. He would good-naturedly turn such inquiries aside (Russian agriculture was a sad joke) by poking the bellies of two plump farmers. Capitalism, he said, feeds it workers very well. Then he grinned his baby-faced grin and poked himself in his porky belly. And so does communism feed its workers well, he said.

Everybody loved it. He might have his plump finger on the trigger of the nuclear bomb, but he was as hammy as Jerry Lewis.

"Boy," Pamela said, "could I use a drink. And a smoke."

Pamela is the girl I've loved since fourth grade. Being that we're both in our mid-twenties now, that's a long time. One other thing I should mention is that Pamela has been in love with Stu Grant since ninth grade. Stu is a rich handsome attorney-at-law who was a golden boy halfback for the Iowa Hawkeyes and whose assets include an inheritance valued at slightly over a million dollars. That he's married now hasn't quelled her ardor much at all.

Two generations ago, her people had a lot of money. The money they lost in the Depression. But they kept their pride and pretensions. Pamela doesn't believe that good girls ever smoke outdoors. Your guess is as good as mine as to *why* good girls don't smoke outdoors. But then your guess is probably also as good as mine as to why Pamela wears a pair of sweet little white gloves just about every time she leaves the house. She wore them today with the blue silk dress with the built-in petticoat and the dark blue leather clutch purse. She was the prototype of all upper-class blond heartbreakers.

"Sounds like a good idea," I said. It'd been a long day. We'd had to get up early for the drive from Black River Falls, and now, with vermilion shadows stretching across the meadows, it was time to go. We'd seen him. I just wish he'd looked more like George Raft, was all.

We left the crowd, passed through the protesters—"Joe Mc-Carthy was right!" one of them shouted, over and over again—and that's when we came upon the bold new black Lincoln of Richard Conners. We were just in time to see his wife Dana—his fifth wife, in case you're counting, and a woman thirty years younger than he—shove Chris Tomlin, and I do mean shove, toward the Lincoln. Chris was an ethereal redhead, very pale, slight and sexual in a quiet but powerful way. She was the wife of Bill Tomlin, the Harvard roommate of Richard Conners. Bill Tomlin had been one of the best political speechwriters in D.C. before going to work for Conners. He'd been along for all of Richard's adventures and was now in charge of organizing his papers for the Conners biography that Bill himself might write.

Both Conners and Tomlin were there and they got between the women immediately. They were all wealthy and attractive people. You didn't expect scenes from them.

This was along the gravel road, where cars were backed up for miles. We'd seen the Lincoln on the highway and ended up parking two cars behind.

"You two get in the car and shut up," Conners snapped. "I'm sick of your damned arguing. You're like a couple of little kids."

He opened up the back door of the Lincoln and practically stuffed Chris inside. Dana went around and got in the front passenger seat.

He had started to get inside the car himself when he saw us approaching. He climbed back out, slammed the door behind him, and said, in a voice comfortable with command, "Tell your girlfriend to go for a walk. I need to talk to you."

"About what?" I resented his tone.

He had one of those profiles made to be chiseled in stone. Better than handsome, he was mythic, especially with his graying locks and his angry blue eyes and his high-rhetoric voice.

"About what?" he said. "About somebody trying to kill me, that's about what. Now can we talk in private or not?"

"I'll go say hi to Dana," Pamela said nervously, and flitted away.

RICHARD CONNERS LEFT Black River Falls in 1931. He went to Harvard, where he completed a master's in political science. Right before the war broke out, he went to work for the State Department. He was soon one of FDR's favorite advisers. He was also brilliant, driven, and contemptuous of just about everything and everybody he encountered. He was, as far as I could gather after slogging through two of his five best-selling books, more of a utopianist than a communist or even socialist. In the meantime, though, his wide circle of friends included many prominent communists and socialists. He even had a very public affair with a Soviet consul's beautiful wife, who killed herself in Anna Karenina fashion after Conners refused to marry her. By that time, he was on his third wife and the divorces were getting expensive.

After the war, Conners worked for Truman, though old Harry never did like or trust him. Conners did a lot of the radio talk shows of the day. His version of things was that he pretty much ran foreign policy and Truman had to get permission before he made any serious foreign policy announcement. All the while he was publishing best-selling books that extolled the virtues of the masses—the kind of thing you'd have if John Steinbeck had written copy to accompany Walker Evans's famous photographs of the Depression—the trouble being that Steinbeck was not only *of* the masses (like Conners), he genuinely *loved* the masses (unlike Conners). Conners spent his public life banging on tables on behalf of the masses, but he spent his private hours in limousines, attending ballet, opera, and movie premieres, and sleeping with the wives of the powerful and famous. His motive seemed to be revenge. By God, I didn't have a silver spoon shoved up my ass the way you did, but I'll get even by turning your spoiled wives into instruments of betrayal.

He was able to sustain his power until another man of the masses came along. For Senator Joseph McCarthy, Richard Conners was an obvious and easy target. All he had to do was remind his ever-growing TV and radio audience that not only did Richard Conners's personal life demonstrate his contempt for American virtues, so did his professional life. He quoted many passages from Conners's books back to him, while Conners sat there looking like a slightly bored duke as played by

Charles Boyer. Two or three times on that first afternoon (you can bet everybody in Black River Falls was watching, McCarthy having convinced the networks to televise his hearings live), Conners corrected McCarthy's grammar and attire ("That suit of yours could stand a cleaning, Senator"). Conners was a strapping, physically powerful man so he never came across as effete, but he did seem arrogant and icy. The last quote McCarthy read was the most devastating. Conners contended that the American press had consciously vilified Stalin, who was, according to Conners, a decent man who only dealt harshly with his political enemies when necessary. "The American press is afraid to portray Joseph Stalin for what he really is—a true man of the people." It was after this that McCarthy hinted he'd given secrets to the Russians.

I still remember that quote and how stupid and infuriating it was. But a good deal of the left was caught up in maintaining Joe Stalin's image as that of a beloved and temperate uncle. Stalin was a butcher on par with Hitler. While I hated the Cold War, I wasn't naïve about Russia or the merciless Soviet regime that ran it, or the proliferation of Russian spies in the United States following the war. The conservatives were paranoid and hysterical about spies; the liberals refused to do anything about them or to even acknowledge their presence.

That was the end for Richard Conners. His State Department tenure ceased with Ike's election, it being unlikely that Conners and John Foster Dulles would become fast friends; Harvard, where he'd been lecturing part-time, declined to invite him back; and his publisher suddenly felt that there was no longer an audience for his books. Such was life during the time of Joe McCarthy. Spying on your fellow American citizens got so bad that the Hearst newspapers started supplying "facts" about local "subversives" in their respective communities.

Conners took to writing mysteries (some good ones) under a pen name and he returned to Black River Falls, where he bought the old Grotte mansion. It was a huge place of native stone, an aerie really, perched above the Iowa River on a red clay mountaintop. He'd been here a year when Trawler College asked him to lecture on political science. He was such a seductive speaker that the college decided to risk the ire of the local political right and make him writer-in-residence.

"C'MON," HE SAID now. "Let's walk."

Despite their political differences—which were vast—my boss, Judge Esme Anne Whitney, who carries a photo of Ayn Rand in her wallet (just kidding), is a friend of Richard Conners. He's a frequent guest at her parties. She considers him something of a social equal, given all his connections. He'd been in her chambers many times when I came in but had never deigned to acknowledge me. I mentioned this to the Judge one day, and she said, "He's a perfect liberal, McCain. He loves the masses but hates people. He figures his love for the downtrodden gives him the right to be a snob and a shit. I, on the other hand, hate the masses but love people." Which was a crock, but I hadn't said anything.

We walked.

All these people, all these cars, you'd think there was a county fair going on. Nice warm September afternoon and all. That tender smoky autumn scent in the piney hills. Hawks swooping down their glide paths. Corn so ripe it's like spilled gold in the fields. Auburn-colored colts running in the high meadows.

Not the afternoon to be talking about murder.

*   *   *

"I STARTED GETTING letters a few weeks ago," Conners said. "Well, not letters exactly; hammers and sickles drawn in blood. Human blood. I had a chemist friend at the college analyze them. Then flat tires and a mysterious fire in my office at the school. And then late-night phone calls. You know the kind. They just hang up. Don't say a word. Last week my dog was poisoned. And last night somebody took a shot at me when I was bringing my horse back from my early evening ride.

"My suspicion is that it's Jeff and that crowd."

Jeff Cronin had been a likable guy when I was growing up. He was several years older but, despite his heroics on the football field, was always decent to us younger kids. The Korean War changed him. (I know we're supposed to call it a police action and all, but around here we call it a war.) Six of our own died over there in the first year. Anyway, Jeff's brother got captured and brainwashed, and Jeff couldn't seem to get past it. The communists had destroyed his brother and they destroyed Jeff, too. Hating communists had become the most important thing in his life.

Conners went on. "They graduated from Trawler and are very prominent alumni and they keep trying to get me fired. That hasn't worked—thanks to Dean Wyman's courage—so maybe now they're trying the more direct approach. I think this has to do with that magazine article, 'The Red Who Got Away.' Walter Winchell gave it a lot of play. They imply I turned state secrets over to the Russians but the State Department covered it up to save embarrassment with that sonofabitch McCarthy coming after them. That article sure didn't do me any good. I mean, back east they know I'm not a communist. But out here—well, you know how people are."

"Hell, yes, I do. We're a bunch of bumpkins and we wouldn't recognize a smear job if you put it up our most delicate orifice."

He looked hard at me. "What the hell are you, a member of the Chamber of Commerce?"

"No, just somebody who likes most of the people in Black River Falls and thinks they're a lot smarter and nicer than you do. Very few people hassled you when you came back here. They took you back as a lost son. The library gave your daughter a job and the women went out of their way to try and make your wife feel comfortable. So don't tell me what a bunch of bigots we are, because it's not true. For every asshole like Jeff Cronin, there are ten very nice people."

"Boy, McCain, are you a hothead."

I shook my head. "I'm not a hothead. I just don't like snobs. And Conners, you're a snob."

He laughed. "You little guys sure have tempers."

"You big guys sure have egos."

He stopped walking. "Now that we've decided not to like each other, how about going to work for me? Esme is quite taken with you."

I'd cooled some. I smiled. "She hides it well."

"Oh, Esme's all right. A bit of a lush, a bit of a poseur—I mean, God, her extended family is riddled with white-collar crooks if you look back far enough; that's where their fortune comes from—but she has a decent heart and a very good mind."

"Which she wastes on Ayn Rand and William F. Buckley."

His laugh was mythic too. He was one of those giant men—like Orson Welles—who should be given to opera capes and top hats. "Now there's something we can finally agree on."

"I'm not sure what I could do for you."

"Try and find out who's after me. This thing is escalating. I'm not a physical coward. But I sure as hell don't like people setting fire to my office and taking shots at me. And then there's something else that happened. It requires more of an explanation than we've got time for now, but—"

I was thinking about telling him I'd make the time when Bill Tomlin approached. Bill and Chris Tomlin lived in a house next to the faux-mansion Conners had bought. Tomlin was, and would always be, the class brain. There was a sad earnestness about the crude haircut, the expensive but wrinkled suit. You never saw him without his briefcase. He had it now, in fact. He also had an occasional tic that jerked his entire head a quarter inch to the right, made more obvious than it had to be by a blue walleye.

"We'd better get going, Richard. You've got that radio interview at nine."

"Oh, thanks for reminding me." He reached out a massive arm and gave Bill a brotherly hug. "I wish the girls got along as well as we did." Then, to me: "What I told you is between us. Not even Esme should know. I don't want that dunce Cliffie Sykes Junior hearing about this."

"Like it or not, he's the law in Black River Falls."

"Yes, and he's also an idiot."

"No argument here."

"And he supports Jeff wholeheartedly. I doubt he'd put much effort into an investigation. Hell, he may be involved himself. Wouldn't surprise me." He turned toward his car. "Gotta go. There's a dinner thing at the school tonight." He looked at me. "I want to give you something tomorrow. Want you to keep it for me."

Then he and Bill Tomlin, big striding brother and shambling little one, headed back toward their fancy car.

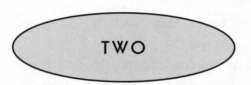

TWO

"Y OU KNOW WHAT I am, McCain?"
      "Yes, I do know what you are: fetching."
"No, I'm serious."
"So am I."
The beautiful Pamela and I were going back home in my red
'51 Ford convertible with the white sidewalls and the extra-
powerful radio that can pull in clear-channel KOMA, the
world's best rock-and-roll station, with no problem at all.
Though the top was still down, and the sky was filled with
those impossible colors only near-dusk can create, a chill was
in the air and I knew that soon enough she'd be asking me to
stop and put the top up. Such are the duties of ragtop owners.
      Pamela had put a sweater over her elegant shoulders. "I was
watching this movie the other night."
      "Uh-huh."
      "With Alexis Smith and Zachary Scott. Did you happen to
see it, by any chance?"
      "Uh-uh."

"Zachary Scott is married and he's got two little daughters, but he's having this affair with Alexis Smith."

"I see." Not sure where this was going.

"*The Other Woman*. That was the name of it."

"Makes sense."

"Well, think about it, McCain."

"Huh?"

"The similarities? Stu and me? He has a wife and two sweet little daughters. So what does that make me?"

"Oh, I see."

"I'm the other woman."

I reached over and took her hand. Sometimes that's OK with her; sometimes it's not. This time it was. "Yeah, I guess you're right. I'm sorry, Pamela."

"So the first thing next morning I called him at the office and said that either he did the right thing and ask his wife for a divorce or it was over for us. I couldn't hurt his wife and daughters anymore."

"And he said what?"

"He said he'd get back to me."

"He'd get back to you? What did he think he was doing, closing on a mortgage?"

"He always talks like that. I never said he was real romantic."

"Apparently not."

"Anyway, I told him if people ever found out, just think what my reputation would be like. Everybody'd think I was a whore." She looked off at the cornfields and pastures and then back at me. "Maybe I *am* a whore."

"You know better than that." Then: "So, did he get back to you?"

"Yes," she said. "He called me last night. When I told him I was going to see Khrushchev with you, he got mad."

"Because of me or Khrushchev?"

"Both. He's jealous of you, though he always says that's ridiculous because you're so short; and his dad is a member of the John Birch Society, so he wouldn't cross the street to see a communist."

I was afraid to ask. "What did he say about leaving his wife?"

She looked at me, and I couldn't ever remember seeing her more lovely. "He said yes, McCain. He said he wants to marry me. I still can't believe it. He's going to tell Donna about us tonight."

THERE'S A GREAT F. Scott Fitzgerald story called "Winter Dreams," in which the protagonist falls in love with this girl when he's barely a teen and loves her throughout his life. He becomes all the things she wanted for a husband: rich, powerful, successful. And yet she always eludes him. She ends up having a pretty terrible life—marrying a faithless alcoholic, losing her looks—and when this is recounted to him many years later he isn't sure what to feel. He still loves her too much to feel good about her dashed hopes. But what he mostly feels is nothing, his care having been blunted by losing her so many times. He wants to cry—maybe for himself; maybe for her; maybe for both of them—but nothing comes. His grief over not having her was something to cling to. Now there is just emptiness.

I guess I felt that way. She didn't gloat. I mean, she knew her happiness meant my doom. So she would move beyond me forever. The worst part of it was Stu. His ambition was to become governor. He stood a good chance. But now he was willing to sacrifice it for Pamela. He loved her as much as I did, maybe more. How could I blame him?

Just at dusk, with clouds and shadows tinted in that mid-western violet, I stopped to put up the top. She used the rest room of the tiny gas station. I leaned against the car, smoking a Lucky, and for just a moment, and utterly without warning, tears stung my eyes. God, I'd loved her for so long. And now it was done.

I'M NOT A drinker. Like my dad, I'm small and I just don't have the capacity. By the time I dropped her off and tooled back downtown, the liquor store was closed. They keep strict hours, and you have to sign for every bottle you take out so the state has a record of it. This is what you get when boozers and teetotalers work out a compromise.

But there were bellhops at all four hotels who could provide you with a bottle for twice what it would cost you at the liquor store. I wasn't even sure I wanted one. But it seemed like the kind of thing Robert Ryan would do in one of his crime movies, and sometimes in my head—and this is sort of embarrassing because I'm going on twenty-six years old—sometimes in my head I'm Robert Ryan. I used to be Gene Autry, but at least then I had an excuse. I was seven years old.

I got a fifth of Old Grand Dad and drove back to my apartment. Mrs. Goldman, the widow who owns the house and lets out two upstairs apartments—I'd call her my landlady but if you ever saw her you'd never call her a landlady—wasn't home, so I knew I'd be drinking alone.

Things got fuzzy pretty quick. I told you I just don't have the capacity. I hauled out some old photos of Pamela, and then I didn't have any trouble crying at all. I had to damned near nail my hand down to keep from calling her and telling her what a mistake she was making. Around two I started vomiting, and the first time I tried to flop into bed I missed and hit the floor face first. Then I vomited some more and then I tried the bed again. I did a little better. I got most of my body on the mattress. The rest is a blank.

"C'MON, NOW, DON'T be a baby."
    "You really didn't have to do this."
    "Yes, I did."
    "Why?"
    "Because you asked me to."
    "I did? When?"
    "When you came down last night."
    "I *came down* last night?"
    "Yes."
    "When?"
    "Maybe four."
    "Oh, my God, I'm sorry."
    "You told me all about Pamela. And then you told me you were afraid you'd never be able to get up in the morning. And that you had too much to do to sleep in. So I said I'd make sure you got up."
    What she'd done was serve me breakfast in bed, Mrs. Goldman. I always say that when Lauren Bacall gets older, she'll look like Mrs. Goldman—if she's lucky. When her husband died and left her this two-story Victorian, people wondered if she'd be able to get along. She's doing just fine, thank you.
    Especially where I was concerned. She had me sitting up in bed drinking coffee, smoking a Lucky, and eating off a breakfast tray that offered three poached eggs, two slices of buttered toast with strawberry jam, and a glass of orange juice.
    My three cats wanted to share the meal. Mrs. Goldman and

I had to fight them off. Tess was the most creative. She started at the foot of the bed and tunneled all the way up, so that her head appeared right next to my toast.

Mrs. Goldman said, "You have to get all this down, Mc-Cain. Isn't your first appointment for nine?"

"Umm-hmm. With the Judge."

"Well, it's eight-fifteen. You still have to take a shower."

"I really appreciate this."

She touched my sleeve. "I was rebounding when I met my husband. I'd loved this guy all the way through college and he wouldn't give me a second look. The first six or seven times I went out with Ken I thought he was the dullest guy I'd ever known. How could anyone compare? But you know, after a couple of months, Ken became my whole life. And he stayed that way for almost thirty years. That'll happen to you, too, McCain. Wait and see."

"I sure hope so."

She stood up. "I hope you're not going to waste that food I've been slaving over for the past half hour."

"Ah. The guilt approach."

"You're darn right," she said. "The guilt approach. Now eat."

I ate.

THREE

If I were a portrait painter—and believe me, there's never any danger of that happening, given the fact that my fifth grade art teacher once delicately asked my mom if I'd ever suffered a head injury—I'd paint Judge Esme Anne Whitney in one of her tailored suits with a nice small white scarf tucked into the neck. In one hand there'd be a Gauloise cigarette burning and in the other a snifter of brandy. She's handsome rather than pretty, though she's damned handsome and damned imposing, something *pretty* rarely is. She's one of those people who'd look upper-crust even if she were starkers. Something in the genes, maybe. She doesn't need clothes to announce her social standing. She's in her early sixties, though she doesn't look it, and God knows she'd never admit it. The Gauloises and the brandy are with her everywhere but in court. I strongly suspect she even imbibes under water, in the swimming pool she had installed two summers ago. She came out here to lend a hand when a relative got in trouble. Her family money ran this town at that time. Somehow the years came and went and she never left, even though the Sykes clan—our visiting family from the land of Hillbillia—took over shortly after the war.

The meeting this morning stretched into an hour, an unlikely length, given the Judge's crowded docket. At any given time, I'm working on three or four investigations for her court. A good thing I got my private investigator's license. It supported my law school sheepskin, which was little more than a bragging point for my family.

I was reporting on the third and final investigation—the Judge had asked me to check out a new merchant's background, which she suspected would be criminal—when Pamela buzzed her from the outer office. Pamela sounded slightly frazzled. Something she rarely sounds.

Pamela gulped and said, "Gosh, Judge, do you know who's on the phone for you?"

The Judge rolled her eyes. I think she chose Pamela as her secretary because Pamela knows how to dress in the eastern fashion and is in all respects a lady. This isn't to say that the Judge has any respect for her. Pamela is an employee and the Judge has no respect for anybody who works for her. I know.

"J. Edgar Hoover!" Pamela said.

"I hope you didn't sound like such a ninny when you were talking to *him*," the Judge said. "Pamela, he calls me all the time. But usually at home in the evening. We're old friends. It's nothing to get excited about. Now put him on the line."

"Yes, ma'am."

Then: "Edgar. Hello, darling. What's the weather like there? . . . Yes, it's a beautiful fall day here, too. How's Clyde? . . . Well, that's very thoughtful of you, Edgar, and I appreciate it. . . . I'll be in New York all Christmas week; I'll just fly down to Washington for your New Year's Eve party. . . . You mean when I was showing you how to rhumba? Don't be silly. I wasn't hurt at all. I was just limping to make a joke! You're a *wonderful* dancer, Edgar. My Lord, everybody knows that. . . . Well, thank you very much for the invitation. But I'm sure we'll talk before then."

She hung up.

"Excuse me if I sound like a ninny too," I said, "but was that really J. Edgar Hoover?"

"No, McCain, it was an imitator I hired just to shake up Pamela." A sip of brandy. A deep drag on the Gauloise. "Of course it was. He's an old family friend." She leaned forward and somehow the angle revealed the girl in the woman. She was suddenly back in sixth grade and whispering a secret to the boy across the aisle. "Between us, he's the most brutal dancer to ever set foot on a floor. I spent twenty minutes teaching him the rhumba and two weeks recovering. My foot probably should've been in a cast. On the other hand, his friend Clyde could give Fred Astaire a few pointers. He's great." Another sip. Another drag. "Now, where were we?"

"I was going to tell you what I found out about Harold Giddins."

"Oh, that's right. But before you do, I want to say that you look terribly hung over this morning."

"I got a bit carried away last night."

"A little fellow like you has to be careful."

"Thank you."

"No offense intended. But you're obviously not a drinker." She said this, taking yet another sip of her brandy. It was 10:32 in the A.M. "Before we get to Giddins, I had a very strange call this morning from Dana Conners. She said Richard talked to you yesterday about somebody trying to kill him."

I hesitated, knowing that Conners didn't want me to acknowledge this to anybody. But I didn't have any choice. "Yes."

"And exactly when were you going to tell me about this?"

"As soon as I thought it was appropriate."

"I'm going to give him some hell for not telling me first, you can bet on that."

Then she did it. First time this morning. Brought her hand up, a rubber band strung between her thumb and forefinger. Like a bow and arrow. She shot the rubber band, and it got me right on the forehead and hung there. The hangover had left me with damp skin that acted as an adhesive.

"There's another reason you shouldn't drink, McCain. Slows your reflexes. You look damned silly with that rubber band on your forehead, believe me. Now swipe it away."

I swiped it away.

"That's the case I want you to concentrate on. Richard's, I mean. As you know, I don't have any liking for his tolerance but we have so many friends in common, he's—"

"He's a Brahmin."

"I beg your pardon."

"He's a peer. Acceptable to your little circle of rich people."

"It's rich people who built this country."

"Yes, on the backs of poor whites, Negroes, Mexicans, and Chinese, mostly."

"Now you sound like Richard."

"I don't care for the man personally, but I do agree with some of his ideas."

"You don't care for Richard? You're both sort of . . . commies, McCain. No offense."

The way she said *commies* was actually sort of cute. Always just the slightest hesitation before saying it. As if she were going to get her mouth washed out with soap as soon as she uttered it.

She said, "Find out what's going on. Dana thinks it's our friends Cliffie and Jeff Cronin."

I laughed. "How does it feel to be on the same side as those two?"

A sip of brandy. "Oh, please. I'm hardly on the same side. About the only thing we have in common is our belief that poor Joe McCarthy got driven out by the liberals."

"Ah, yes. Saint Joe. I'd forgotten."

"You would've mocked Napoleon if you'd lived back then."

"Not to mention Caligula."

She got me again. This rubber band rested on top of my head. "Now that's something you don't see very often."

"No, I've noticed that. Your rubber bands rarely land up top. Maybe we should inform the people at Ripley's Believe It Or Not."

"You really shouldn't drink, McCain. Your reflexes are awful. I rarely get you twice in one day. Not anymore, anyway."

I stood up and went to the door.

"I won't try to hit you again today. It'd be like shooting fish in a barrel."

"Your largesse knows no bounds." I put my hand on the knob.

"It's very frustrating when you're hung over, McCain. You take away one of the few pleasures our little burg here affords me. You could think of me and *my* needs once in a while, for God's sake, couldn't you?"

BIG-CITY INVESTIGATORS RELY on private sources of information far more than they do on legwork. A town our size doesn't have stool pigeons per se, but it does have a group of old folks who know more about what's going on than any cop, county attorney, or newspaper reporter. And, conveniently enough, they can be found most days around a bridge table out at the Sunset Care Home.

You hear a lot of arguments against nursing homes, but this one actually has a reason to exist—besides the greed of the owners, I mean. The eighteen souls who live there all had the misfortune of losing their children down the years so there is nobody else to take care of them. The facility, a long, barrack-like building, is set at the base of piney hills. There's a clean creek running nearby, horses in a pasture, picnic tables and an outdoor grill, and some nice hiking trails for those so inclined. The staff is competent, friendly, and actually likes the people it serves.

I got there, as I usually do, just at noon so I wouldn't inter-rupt any TV shows. It's visits that keep these folks apprised of all the gossip, rumor, and scuttlebutt I find useful. These folks talk to a wide range of people every day—doctors, delivery-men, workmen, ministers, visitors, each other—and they listen carefully and retain what they hear. And then they begin to speculate among themselves about what they've heard. And they start to form impressions. You could call it gossiping, I suppose, but it's subtler and more refined than that. It's the kind of deduction that detectives and DA's make when they're putting together a case.

You have to be careful and make sure you get around to every one of them. You don't want to leave anybody out. I also bring small gifts from time to time.

I hadn't talked to Helen Grady in some time. Helen fre-quently eats alone if she's reading one of her Mickey Spillane novels. Helen, eighty-two, a grandmother seven times over, is Spillane's most faithful fan. She's read all the books many times but says her memory is just bad enough that by the time she starts over again she's forgotten the plots.

The lunchroom was sunny. The windows were open. The repast today was hamburger, fresh-cut green beans, peaches in syrup, and a slice of cherry pie. It made me hungry.

All but Helen were divided up at two long tables. Tom

Swanson winked at me and said, "Helen's finishin' up *One Lonely Night*. That's where the woman turns out to be a man."

And then they started talking about the difficulty of using bifocals. I walked over to the only table for two. "Hi, Helen."

She looked up from her paperback. "Hey, it's the gumshoe."

Helen loved hard-boiled talk. She wore a flowered house-dress, pince-nez reading glasses, pancake makeup that looked like real batter, and lipstick that told me she hadn't been wearing eyeglasses when she'd put it on. "Sit down and take a load off."

"Thanks."

"So how you be, shamus?"

"Pretty good, I guess."

"Any damsels in your life?"

"Not so's you'd notice."

She paused, then waggled the paperback at me. "Hammer's in big trouble. Commies. And they've got Velda."

"Let me know how it comes out."

She frowned at the glass sitting next to her cleaned-up luncheon plate. "All they serve in this joint is iced tea. What a gal wouldn't give for a shot of the real stuff."

"Real stuff?"

"Pepsi."

"Ah."

"Doctor said it's got too much acid for my stomach." She dog-eared the book. "A stoolie gets lonely, gumshoe. Here you are, six or seven times the last couple months, making the rounds, and you don't visit your favorite stoolie."

"I'll try and do better. I promise."

A melancholy came over her wide white face. She looked teary. "Husband's birthday today. He woulda been eighty-eight."

"I'm sorry."

"Had this damn thing on his neck. Big ugly thing. Kept telling me it was a goiter. Goiter my foot, I said. Took me three years to get him to the doc's and by then it was too late. I shoulda pushed him more." She was starting to cry. That was one reason I didn't visit her as often as I once did. She phased in and out of the past. Sometimes it seemed to attack her.

"Did I ever tell you that before? About that thing on Fred's neck?"

"I think you mentioned it once or twice, Helen."

She sighed. "I ever tell you why he married me?"

"I don't think so." She had, of course. Many times.

"I was the Corn Queen of 'Twenty-nine. I ever show you a picture of me back then?"

"Yeah. Once."

"I was somethin'." She really had been something. But time is never kind.

"But even with bein' Corn Queen and all, I still had to chase him. He didn't chase me. Oh, no. Wasn't a gal in the whole county who hadn't cocked their hats for him. He'd inherited better'n nine hundred acres from his dad and didn't owe a dime on 'em. And he was good-lookin' besides. You think the gals weren't after him?"

"I'm sure they were."

"He married me because I could sing, he said. His mom had this old piano, and she'd been dead a long time and nobody had sung in the house for years. So one day I was out there and I sat down at the piano and sang some of the popular songs, and that's when he said he fell in love with me. We had three kids, and his favorite nights were when we'd all get around the piano and sing." She choked back sudden tears. "I kept tellin' him and tellin' him about that damn thing on his neck. But he just wouldn't do anything about it."

I gave her my white handkerchief. She turned a good deal of it damp. I told her to keep it. I said, "Feel like playing stool pigeon?"

She grinned. "Sure, gumshoe."

"You hear any word on Richard Conners?"

"What kind of word?"

"That somebody might want to hurt him."

"A lot of people want to hurt him."

"Like who?"

"Jeff and that crowd. They're trying to get him kicked off the Trawler faculty."

"Anybody else but that bunch?"

"You'd think they'd be proud of him. He's the most prominent man ever come from this town. I don't agree with his politics, but I'm proud of him anyway." She spoke for the majority of citizens, I'm sure. Then, as if the question had just now registered: "I haven't heard of anybody trying to get him, though. 'Less it'd be a husband."

"A husband?"

"Our Richard gets around."

"He does?"

"Do I have to draw you a picture?"

"You mean sleeping with?"

She laughed, and the laugh exploded into a cough. I had to get some iced tea down her before the hacking stopped. She was so big and yet so delicate—death is always imminent at her age and state of health—that the kind of useless pity you feel for the dying came over me. All I can say is that on the other side everybody damned well better have brand-new cars to drive and new episodes of *Gunsmoke* to watch three nights a week.

"Who told you this?" I said, when she was all right again.

"I'm a stoolie, gumshoe. I don't reveal my sources."

"C'mon, Helen."

"The candy machine guy."

"How'd he know about it?"

"He talks to a lot of people on his route."

"Any specific names?"

"None that he shared."

"He reliable, you think?"

"At least fifty percent of the time."

I laughed. "Now there's a recommendation."

"Conners a client of yours?" she asked.

"Not exactly. I mean, we haven't made anything official."

"That's the kind of thing can get a man killed. You should tell your client that."

I SPENT THE middle hours of the afternoon finishing work on one of the Judge's other cases. This one involved a property dispute between two lonely old widowers whose only pleasure in life was harassing their neighbors, whom they resented for having actual lives. I got the two of them to sit down in a tavern. One preferred to talk without his dentures in, which is always pleasant, and the other kept passing the kind of deadly gas the Germans used in the First World War. The Judge had decided to bring back some old traffic charges against one and some old drunk-and-disorderly fines against the other—unless they agreed to drop their case. The Judge was too busy for such Mickey Mouse antics, I'd been told to tell them, and it was past time these two dipshits started acting their age, which was somewhere around ninety.

"She really called us that?" one of them asked.

"Dipshits, you mean?"

"Yeah."

"Yeah, that's *exactly* what she called you."

"That gal's got some mouth on her, don't she?" he said. They agreed to drop the suit.

My next stop was a phone booth outside the service station where I get my Ford worked on. I'd noticed a strange little squeal when I turn right abruptly. I take better care of my car's health than I do my own. I had Gil run it up on the hoist for a quick peek. Gil had been in the news lately because—in response to a competitor of his who stuffed twelve college freshmen into a phone booth—Gil had stuffed forty college freshmen into a Volkswagen. Gil was a mechanic on bombers back in the war. He's the Toscanini of motors. He told me he couldn't keep up with all the business that came in as a result of the VW thing. I'm not sure that's the greatest recommendation for a service garage, but in Gil's case it worked out.

I'VE GOT THIS little office stuck in the back of a large building that keeps changing businesses. Right now, it's a paint store. My office has its own small parking lot and entrance. A lot of law firms these days play what they call Muzak, very bland instrumental music kept very low. It's supposed to keep spirits (and productivity) high.

I wonder what the inventor of Muzak would think of Jamie Newton's form of Muzak: namely, Jerry Lee Lewis's "Great Balls of Fire" played very loud. I know my clients sure like it ("How the hell come you've got rock-and-roll blaring in the background every time I call there, McCain, and who's that idiot you've got answering the phone?").

A small-town attorney gets paid in many ways. Food is a favorite. Last summer I settled a bill in exchange for a quarter of beef. I get free lunches at a restaurant for defending an arson case brought against them. I did some work for a local farmer, and I'm looking at five years' worth of freshly picked vegetables.

Lloyd Newton, a worker out at the glass-making plant, was the first to ever give me his daughter.

Jamie is seventeen, sexy, freckled, cute, and totally incompetent. She fashioned herself after all the bad girls you see on those jailbait paperback covers. You know, the white socks, the penny loafers, the tight dungarees rolled up to display the elegant calf, the tight white blouse with collar turned up and bullet bra pointing the fetching breasts toward ecstasy, the erotically lipsticked mouth, and the jarringly innocent ponytail.

I walked in and went over to the radio and turned down the sound. I like Jerry Lee Lewis well enough but not during working hours.

She was too busy typing to notice me. I'm a two-finger typist myself. Jamie is even more energy-efficient. She only types with one finger, which she can do with no trouble at all while making a huge pink plastic dome of the bubble gum she constantly chews. It's like watching a frog's throat sac expand and diminish all day.

She hit a final key and said, "There!"

Then, like a teen princess awakening, she looked up and said, "Gee, Mr. C! I didn't even hear you come in! I was really working on this business letter!"

Savvy, no; enthusiasm, yes.

And then she handed me the letter. I'd scribbled it out for her in longhand. She'd typed it for me.

   Mr. Ardur Shermin
   Presidunt
   Sherman Farm Implents

Sepotember 24, 1959

Dear Mr Shermun,

My accountent informs me that your account with my law office is in serus arrears. While I don't generally turn things ovr to a collection agency, I'm afraid I must consder doing so now unless you make arranggements with me within thre working days.

You will find my phone numer and address on this leterhead. Please avail yourself of my offer or I will be farced to take other action.

Sincerely,
Samm McCainn

"And it only took me an hour and a half!"

"Gosh," I said, "that beats your old record, doesn't it?"

"Yeah!" she said proudly. Then yawned. "Boy, that just about wore me out!" She was talking, as she always did, in sentences that ended in exclamation points. Or, as she'd type it out for me, in exxclametion pointes!

"Well, I can certainly see why you'd be tired after work like this."

"Really?" she said. "Because you know, sometimes I get this feeling you don't like think I'm doing, you know, a real good job!"

"Are you kidding? This office hasn't been the same since you started coming here."

"Well, Dad thought you might be mad about my accidentally flicking my cigarette ashes on some of your papers that time. You remember? When they caught fire?"

"Oh, dimly. Way in the back of my mind."

She yawned again. "You think I could take a break? Maybe get a cherry Coke or somethin'? That typing really took it out of me."

"A break? After work like this? You should get a whole week off!" She had me talking in exxclamation pointes now too. Or, if you prefer, two.

Then I was taking her elbow and escorting her to the door and stuffing a dollar and a half in her hand. "I don't need to see you till next week. This is just a little bonus."

"Next week! But Dad said I was supposed to come in every day!"

"But you've done such a great job, you've finished all your work for the week!"

"Oh, great! Wait till I tell Dad! He'll be surprised! He thinks I'm kinda stupid!"

"Well, the next time I see him, I'm gonna set him straight on that one!"

"See ya, Mr. C!"

"See ya, Jamie!"

After she was gone, I went back to my desk, sat down, opened the middle left drawer, and took out the sheet of typing paper that read JAMMIE. HOURS. She'd even managed to mis-type her own name. While she had a decent heart, a secretary she wasn't. I couldn't tell her old man that, of course. Who wants to hear that his daughter is a dope? It's one thing for *you* to say it about your daughter but quite something else for anybody else. She'd been in an hour and a half today so I wrote down 6. The deal was she was to work a hundred hours and our debt would be canceled. I was adding hours on every chance I got.

Then the hangover caught up with me. Coffee and cigarettes had held it at bay for most of the day but then, as I sat at my desk, I felt my eyes start to close and my entire body collapse in on itself. No energy left at all.

I took the phone off the hook. I took the cushion off the chair and put it on the floor. I took the blanket from the closet—two blankets, actually, one bottom, one top—undressed, laid myself down, and went to sleep. There are some hangovers only the sandman can cure. And from time to time, I'm called upon to take an extended nap on the floor in order to rally myself and better serve my clients.

An hour later, I was awakened by a gentle knock on my door. I said, "Just a minute," trotted down the hall to the bathroom we shared, splashed water on my face, squirted Ipana in my mouth, brushed my teeth with my finger, and climbed into my clothes.

My instant impression was that he was drunk. He didn't look as regal or imposing as he usually did, either. Maybe it was because he was reeling back and forth on his heels, the way a drunk does before he lands on his face. But then, registering almost simultaneously, was the lurid red hammer and sickle somebody had painted on his forehead. He wore a heavy tweed topcoat, and when he started falling toward me, his bloody lips parted and fresh blood came out in a dark red gush. He said something—or maybe just *tried* to say something—just before I got him under the shoulders and began dragging his considerable body inside.

I had just gotten the bulk of him across the threshold when I looked up and saw Jamie standing on the steps behind him. "I forgot to tell ya that Mr. Conners called and said he'd be stopping by, Mr. C." She looked down at him and said, "Guess I'm a little late, huh?" And then: "I think I'm gonna upchuck, Mr. C."

FOUR

I secretly think I'm Robert Ryan and Cliffie Sykes Jr. secretly thinks he's Glenn Ford. Glenn always wears khaki uniforms and a version of a campaign hat whenever he plays a modern-day lawman. The only trouble is I'm too short to be Ryan and Cliffie's too round to be Ford. His dad made a lot of money building training airstrips for the government during the war. Before then he'd been just another cracker from down South who had shirttail kin up here and decided to give it a go. In the late forties, Judge Whitney's family was running things. Cliffie Sr. did the unthinkable—he bought the town. Or, rather, bought off the town. He was able to install his own people on all levels of city government—except for Esme's seat. That was an appointment they couldn't get around. Since then, the Judge has dedicated her judicial life to showing up Cliffie Jr. for the puffed-up incompetent he is. For his twenty-first birthday, his daddy gave him the choice of any appointed job he wanted. If you were secretly Glenn Ford, what office would *you* take? Ladies and gentlemen, I give you our chief of police.

"So there you are," Cliffie Jr. said, twenty minutes later, really enjoying himself.

"So there I am."

"Asleep on the floor."

"That's what I said."

A deputy snickered.

"In the middle of the afternoon."

"In the middle of the afternoon."

"In your boxers."

"I wear jockeys."

This time the deputy only smirked.

Cliffie aimed this one right at the most appreciative of the four of us in my office: "You think this is how big-time lawyers operate, McCain?"

The deputy guffawed. A guffaw isn't something you often hear in modern polite society. But there he was, this gink in a tan uniform, guffawing the hell out of Cliffie's remark.

"I wouldn't know."

Cliffie winked at the deputy. "You can be sure your secret is safe with us, right, Roger?"

And then Deputy Roger Weed performed the impossible, a quadruple masterpiece all at the same time: a snicker-laugh-smirk-wink. My reputation would be safe at least until Deputy Weed got out the door.

You hear about McCain?

What'd he do this time?

Cliffie Jr. caught him sleeping on the floor of his office during working hours.

You're kidding.

Nope, and he had some broad with him, too.

Some broad?

Yeah, and Cliffie says when he walked in, the broad didn't

*even put her clothes on right away. Just lit up a cigarette, calm
as you please. Cliffie said the way she was actin', so brazen
and all, he's pretty sure she's a commie.*

"So let's talk about our friend over there."

He meant Richard Conners, of course, who was under a
sheet on a stretcher. Doc Novotny, the only tolerable member
of the Sykes clan, was on his way to perform his sterling best
as county coroner.

"I thought we went through it all. I opened the door and
there he was."

"Were you expecting him?"

"He called Jamie while I was out. Said he'd be stopping by."

"Jamie, huh?" He winked at Roger Weed again. "You better
remember how old she is, McCain. Wouldn't want to see you
get into any kind of trouble."

Or trbble, as Jamie would type it.

"You don't have to worry about that."

"He a client of yours, was he?"

"I assume that's why he wanted to see me."

"He say why?" Cliffie loves pressuring me with stupid questions and I love confusing him, which doesn't, believe me, make
me work hard enough to break a sweat on a day when it's 102
degrees in the shade. There's just one thing about Cliffie. True,
he's a racist bigoted bully, but you tend to forget that when
you see him with his little daughter, who has spina bifida. He's
so purely loving at that moment you think it's somebody in a
Cliffie disguise. I can't figure it out, how anyone can have two
such disparate parts. But as my dad says, life is like that sometimes.

"He said he thought somebody might be trying to kill him."

If I hoped that might get a big reaction, it didn't. Cliffie said,
"Lot of people around here wanted to kill him. He was a commie."

"He wasn't a commie."

"Oh, yeah, I'd expect you to say that. You're sort of a commie yourself. I seen you out there that day with all them colored people."

"We were picketing a restaurant that always made Negroes eat in the back."

"I don't have a prejudiced bone in my body, McCain, but I'll tell you one thing you don't know about the colored. You can trick 'em real easy. And that's just what the commies are doin'. The colored, they think they're doin' one thing—they're always hollerin' about their civil rights and stuff—but they're really doin' somethin' else. What they're really doin' is what the commies want 'em to do. And commies mean Jews. You read me?"

"I read you."

"Used to be the Catholics was tryin' to take over this country, but they couldn't pull it off it so they handed it off to the Jews. Now the Jews are tryin' it and they use the colored to help 'em."

"That's the truth, McCain," Deputy Roger Weed said solemnly, "whether you think so or not."

I looked over at Conners. "He wasn't a commie. I admit he wasn't real easy to like, but I think deep down he was really concerned about the average person getting a better deal."

Cliffie smiled sourly at his deputy. "Ain't that just what the commies say they're doin'?"

"You better listen to him, McCain. This is a man who's put a lot of brain hours into readin' up on commies. Plus he sees *I Was a Communist for the FBI* ever' time it's on at the drive-in."

"Me 'n the missus never miss it," Cliffie said.

But I'm going to stop here. You can pretty much write the rest of the dialogue yourself. Before Conners's wife and brother get here, that is. Cliffie sounded as if he wanted to present a medal to the killer; guy had done the town, the county, the state, the country a favor. He didn't even ask me many more questions about what Conners might have wanted to tell me. Or if he'd hinted at the name of his killer. He just said that commies came to bad ends and he didn't need any more proof than that dead guy across the room there.

Let's pick up the scene about twenty minutes later. The room has three more people in it now, including Doc Novotny. Now, while Doc's medical degree comes from an institution called (and I'm not kidding) the Cincinnati Citadel of Medinomics, he actually seems to know what he's doing most of the time.

But let's skip past Doc coming in and get to the part where Conners's mother and brother are standing on the threshold, staring at the shape beneath the sheet on the stretcher. You can see right away where Richard Conners got his looks. Even at seventy, Dorothy Conners is a damned good-looking and imposing woman. The cliché is that it's all in the genes and bones, and you know what? I think this particular cliché is true. Look at her. Those cheekbones, that fierce but elegant nose, and those blue eyes, so much furious intelligence and sexuality in the eyes. Almost as much as in the erotic mouth. Not even the gray hair or the wrinkles around eyes and mouth can diminish the ferocity of her appeal. But aside from the face, she's her age in terms of fashion. Unremarkable blue dress beneath unremarkable black coat. Plain black purse. Scuffed black walking shoes. White anklets.

God help you if you made her angry. She'd stand up in church or at the city council meeting or in a five-and-dime to denounce you if she believed you were in any way taking advantage of your fellow man. There's a hard prairie woman in her, the woman who trekked west in a wagon that broke down every other day, who felled trees alongside her husband, who adjusted to living in a soddy rather than a cabin; the woman who fought off Indians, rattlesnakes, cholera; the woman who watched half her children die before age eight, worked far longer hours than her farmer husband, and saw many of her prairie woman friends commit suicide before age thirty. She is against the death penalty, for liquor by the drink, for the right to have an abortion, for integration, for the right to put "dangerous" books into the libraries. And while I agreed with her on many issues—just as I'd agreed with her son Richard—she was something of a scold, with a scold's self-righteousness and smugness. She was also tireless once she got going. All of which may explain how Richard turned out as he did.

Cliffie stopped lecturing me about commies when Dorothy Conners walked into the room without acknowledging any of us and stood over the sheet hiding her son. She pulled it back just far enough to see his face. Then she quickly covered it up again. Her expression was hard, controlled. No sign of grief, not even anger.

Then she looked at Cliffie and said, "I'm giving you twenty-four hours to find out who killed him, Sykes. And if you don't have somebody in jail by then, I'm calling the governor. He's a Democrat and owes me a favor. I'll have him send out some state investigators to work independent of you on this."

"Now wait a minute here, Mrs. Conners," Cliffie said, starting to rise from his chair. "You don't have no right to—"

She looked at me. "I need to get some groceries." Then, to Cliffie: "Twenty-four hours, Cliffie. I mean it."

About the last thing Cliffie liked was being called Cliffie. About the second to the last thing he liked was being threatened.

"Bitch," Cliffie said, when she'd gone. "Fucking bitch."

FIVE

Richard Conners was unduly fond of his Jaguar. It was an easy way to demonstrate his social superiority, as only a true liberal could. People would stand on the corner and point to it the way they would at a UFO.

But Conners had always been anxious about parking it. Somebody might run into it. Or break into it. So he made this deal with Mike's Auto Repair. Mike Burleigh owned an empty garage in the same alley where he had his repair shop. It was downtown, so it was a convenient parking spot. Conners rented the small garage from him. Whenever he drove into town, he ran his car in there and locked the garage door, and the Jag, all sleek and silver, was safe.

I doubted if Cliffie had checked out the garage yet. Maybe he didn't even know about Conners's arrangement with Mike.

I walked over there. I wanted to take full true measure of the gentle autumn day, but I couldn't quite. I kept seeing Conners falling through my doorway, dead.

When you're a kid, alleys are about the neatest places there are except maybe for cellars and basements. Alleys are perfect for any kind of game you want to play: war, cowboys-and-Indians, even science-fiction games. Alleys have neat places to hide, neat places to fall dead and give little dying speeches like they do in the movies, and neat places to jump off of. Alleys are universes unto themselves.

That's when you're a kid. When you're older, you tend to smell the garbage in the cans, and notice the town drunk sleeping off another sad bender behind a couple of empty crates, and be slightly offended by all the dirty words kids have scrawled on the garage walls.

This alley dated back to at least the turn of the century. Dozens of businesses had come and gone here in that time. It was narrow and without shade because there were no trees. The backs of the two-story wooden buildings gave it the feeling of a small canyon. The liveliest place was Mike Auto's Repair. Auto shops tend to be noisy places. I went directly to the garage Conners had rented. Nothing special about it at all. A one-stall garage. There was a clasp where a Yale lock had held the door in place. But the lock was gone. The door opened sideways. I pulled it far enough to get inside.

The interior smelled of faded sunlight, car oil, the feces of a dozen different creatures. It was the kind of garage where a lot of us got our first kisses. Little boys and girls playing together and then experimenting with kisses, and maybe a little more, the way couples on TV were always doing it.

I looked around. Except for the Jaguar, nothing notable presented itself. I saw a spider in a web, a caterpillar crawling along the edge of a two-by-four, a robin dead and mummified in a corner. An odd little nook of existence.

The handprint wasn't hard to find once I got close. Three of them, in fact: handprints made in blood. I could picture Richard, after being shot, reeling from the car, falling against the wall here. Leaving his print, his palm wet from touching his wound.

I spent a few minutes there and then went over to Mike Burleigh's place. Mike had been a classmate of mine from kindergarten through high school. We'd never been close friends, but I'd see him at all the auto shows and stock car races and that was enough to make us friendly. He went to work for the guy who'd once been the dominant auto repair man in town. A couple years ago, Mike had bought him out. Now he was the main man.

Mike was bulky in his white DX coveralls. Not only were the coveralls greasy, so was his bald head. A wriggle of black grease looked like a birth defect right across the center of his pink dome.

"Hey, counselor."

"Hi, Mike. I take it you heard about Richard Conners."

He frowned. "That's the kind of thing scares the shit out of you, isn't it? I mean, Des Moines or Cedar Rapids or one of the river towns—sure, stuff happens there. But Black River Falls?" He shook his head again.

"You didn't happen to talk to Conners today, did you?"

"Not today. Sometimes, he brings his car in for me to work on. Says he's finally getting me trained to work on a Jag. Personally, I wouldn't want the damned thing. Too much trouble."

"But he didn't come in today?"

"Nope. Just pulled into the garage and walked to wherever he was going. Which is what he usually does—did, I guess I should say now."

"You didn't hear a gunshot by any chance, did you?"

"You kidding?"

Wrenches clanging when they hit the concrete floor, Chuck

Berry on the radio, mechanics shouting back and forth in ech-oing voices—there was my answer.

Before I went back to my office and got my car, I walked up and down the alley three times. I had no idea what I was looking for exactly. The backs of the various retail shops of-fered me no help at all.

I TOOK THE long way home, which led me past Trawler College, nine red-brick buildings built over a twenty-year pe-riod, sitting on a vast wooded hill. There had always been a fortresslike air about the place, as if it wanted to repel all the nonsense and vulgarity to be found in the town below. If you believed its brochure, Trawler was considered "the Harvard of small midwestern liberal arts colleges." The claim would have been stronger if it had cited a source. Presumably, the Trawler English professors wouldn't let you get away with such stuff.

This was the year that college kids discovered folk music. Or the Tin Pan Alley version of it, anyway. The Kingston Trio was the hottest act on campuses, and boys and girls alike wore a lot of bold-striped shirts in their honor. A harmless diver-sion—it was better than listening to Fabian, anyway—until they started updating and sanitizing some of the old labor songs. Then I wanted to reach for my gun. Those songs were based on the lives of immigrants who had struggled and suf-fered all their lives. Turning them into hummable sap for col-lege kids irritated me. For the most part, Trawler students are rich Chicago kids who flunked out of or couldn't get into other schools. They drive cars far superior to those of most town folks and make frequent trips to nearby Cedar Rapids and Iowa City (we're pretty much between the two), where they spend their parents' money with abandon. This isn't to say they're bad kids or stupid kids. Not at all. It's just that they've

never been very cordial to the people of Black River Falls, and
that has left some resentment in town. As for the school itself,
I'd taken two night school courses there. The instructors were
damned good. I might even have gone there for my BA but my
folks could never have afforded it. I went to the U of Iowa.

Folk music seemed to come from every dorm window. I
wanted to hear Chuck Berry or Little Richard or Elvis. I needed
my sinus passages cleared.

Even though dinnertime was near, and most of the faculty
should be home, there were two or three little clutches of them
in the lobby area of the first building I came to. They ran to
crew cuts, Hush Puppies, button-down shirts, black-rimmed
eyeglasses, cardigans, and dark trousers. A few pipes, mostly
cigarettes. One Negro, a handful of women. A few of them
recognized me and nodded. Most of them spoke low, the way
you would in a funeral home. You could tell they'd been
shocked, not in any dramatic way but in a quieter, more lasting
way, perhaps. One of their own—no matter how much they
might have disliked him—had been killed. One more measure
of their own mortality.

A tall woman in a blue crew-neck sweater, Peter Pan collar,
and a gray skirt came over to me: Nan Richmond. I'd helped
her with some vandalism she'd suffered. Turned out to be an
ex-boyfriend. Her hair had started to streak gray in the two
years since I'd last seen her.

"Oh, God, McCain," she said, "it's so awful. He died in
your office?"

I nodded. "Though he was pretty much dead when he got
there."

"I understand he drove. How could he have?"

"He kept his Jaguar in a garage a block away—whenever
he came downtown, I mean. He was always afraid somebody

would run into it. My guess is somebody was waiting for him in the garage."

"That damned car of his." Shook her head. "A hick in a fancy car like that." She glanced over at the black professor. "Nigger rich, if you know what I mean. Same difference."

"I guess I never thought of him as a hick."

"You never really get over the circumstances you were born into. I can't. Nice middle-class Irish Catholic girl from Long Island. I keep trying to leave all my prejudices behind and be more sophisticated, but it's never easy." She smiled. "Parents are like Jesuits. Once they get ahold of you, they never let go." Then: "Oh, Jeez, got to run. My little one's at the baby-sitter." People figured, her being a college prof and a divorcée at that, she'd be easy to get into bed. I've got two bottles of wine and a whole lot of begging to say otherwise. I guess I've never had much luck with the so-called "easy" ones, but then, come to think of it, I haven't had much luck with the "hard" ones either.

I drifted down the hall. Nobody paid any special attention because the men's room was down there around the corner. So was Conners's office. I figured that Cliffie, being Cliffie, probably hadn't thought to seal his office for evidence. That would be too much like actual modern-day law enforcement. And I was right. The short hall had two offices on one wall, an office and a men's room on the other. There was an EXIT sign above the door ahead of me. The ideal office setup. You could sneak out without anybody seeing you.

I saw a very pretty young Negro woman slowly twisting a knob on a door. She was unaware of me at first. She gave the impression of sneaking in. I wondered why. When she saw me, she jumped back from the door and said, "Oh, poor Dr. Conners." She wore a white frilly blouse and a tan skirt with argyle knee socks. With her tortoise-shell eyeglasses, she looked modern and imposing. "I'm Margo Lane. I am—was—his student assistant." Her dark eyes glistened with tears; her perfume gave off an intoxicating heat. "I'm sorry. I need a cup of coffee and a cigarette." She gave a startled little cry and pushed past me.

Between the offices on the west wall was a bulletin board thumbtacked with a variety of colorful brochures offering student scholarships, study vacations, summer jobs, and enlistment in all the armed forces. The draft hung heavy on every young man's mind. It was why I'd joined the National Guard. Ike was sending advisers to a place called Vietnam, but it didn't look like it would become anything serious. It was probably a good time to enlist and get it out of the way.

I heard a chair scrape against the floor on the other side of Conners's closed door and knew something was wrong. Could be his wife or mother, but I guessed otherwise.

I needed some of Helen Grady's hard-boiled talk to get me in the mood for what I was about to do. But I figured the best—probably, only—weapon I had was surprise.

The door was unlocked, which helped. I flung it inward and there he was, hunched over Conners' desk, pulling out a drawer.

He managed to look totally unperturbed. "Hi," he said. "Help you with something?"

"Yeah," I said, "you can tell me who you are and what you're doing here."

"Oh, I'm sorry." He slid the drawer closed and stood up. He was a city fellow, vaguely military. Even with the gray Brooks Brothers suit, the white oxford shirt, and the red-gray-black regimental striped tie—military. He had a lean, angular, feral face. The mouth was too thin and the ears were slightly pointed. He had great teeth. They sparkled. He was thirty or so. "I'm a cousin of the Conners family."

"I see."

"And you are?"

"I'm Sam McCain. I was working for Conners."

"Good for you."

He didn't make a fuss of it. Simply brought it out of a very secretive shoulder holster. A Luger, for God's sake. "If you've got half a brain, hayseed, this gun should be scaring the shit out of you."

"It'd make a hell of a lot of noise."

"Yeah, but you wouldn't be around to hear it."

"So who are you?"

He had a nice grin. Like on TV. But it was a cold grin, the same kind of cold amusement as in the gray eyes. "You fucking farm boys. Whaddaya think I'm gonna do? Hand you my ID and write down my home phone number?"

"I'd appreciate it if you would."

Then he said: "Wait a minute. You're the lawyer he talked to. When you were seeing Khrushchev."

"Were you there?"

"No. And it's a good thing I wasn't. Would've taken every ounce of self-control I had not to shoot that sonofabitch."

"Khrushchev or Conners?"

He grinned. "Both." Then: "Take two steps back and close the door. Real easy. Then take two steps forward and put your hands above your head."

"We going to do some calisthenics, are we?"

"You're pretty bright for a shitkicker."

"You're pretty friendly for a psycho."

He laughed. He actually laughed. Then he motioned with the gun the way they do in the movies. I took two steps back and closed the door gently. I had no thought of escape. I had no doubt he'd shoot me on the spot and worry about his escape afterward. Then I took two steps forward and put my hands above my head.

I had never been hit by anything so hard in my life. It did more than double me over, it felt as if it had tripled me over. One punch into my sternum. I went to my knees. I fell to my face. I couldn't see. I couldn't hear. I felt nauseated.

He went back to searching through drawers. A couple times, he laughed and said, "How you doin', shitkicker? I figured you country boys could take it better'n that."

Standing up took a lot of effort. I pushed through the pain. He kept glancing at me, making sure I was still sufficiently disabled. Now he was going through a closet. "You better hope I find what I'm looking for, hayseed. Because otherwise I start in on you again."

I want to give you something tomorrow. Want you to keep it for me.

In the chaos of the past few hours, I'd forgotten what Conners had said to me yesterday at the Khrushchev visit. *Want you to keep it for me.* Was this what the tough guy was looking for? And, just maybe, could it also be the same thing Conners might have been murdered for? And, if so, what the hell was it?

I stood upright. My breathing was almost regular again. Watching him, I realized I wanted to kill him. Literally. I don't have thoughts like that very often and didn't know what to do with them when I had them. He was right, I was just a shitkicker, and shitkickers don't go around killing people. But in his case, I'd make an exception. He'd hurt my body a lot but even more he'd hurt my pride. The body heals; pride doesn't.

He was just closing the closet door—"Looks like you 'n me need to have a talk, hayseed—" when the office door opened and there stood Cliffie.

For the first and only time I was happy to see him. I wanted him to throw this bastard in jail and keep him there for a good long time. He'd broken into Conners's office, if nothing else.

I'd just opened my mouth to tell Cliffie about him when the tough guy said, "Hey, Cliff, we still on for that steak dinner tonight?"

"You're damned right we are," Cliffie said. "The missus went to the beauty parlor and everything."

"Too bad I don't have my own missus along," the tough guy said.

Cliffie said, "See you've met McCain."

"Not exactly." The tough guy revealed his teeth again and pushed his hand out to shake.

I kept both my hands at my sides. "Arrest this prick."

"McCain," Cliffie said, as if I'd finally lost my mind, "do you know who this man is?" I heard something rare in Cliffie's voice. Reverence. This was somebody Cliffie actually admired.

"Yeah, I know who he is. He's the guy who broke into Conners's office."

"And got a little rough," the tough guy said. "I think I hurt his feelings. You know how sensitive short people are."

Cliffie smiled. "Sorry I missed that part of it. I get a little rough with him every once in a while myself." Then: "For the record, McCain, the man you're insulting is an FBI agent."

"Bullshit," I said.

"What's that supposed to mean?" Cliffie said.

"It means he's not an FBI agent."

"Oh, no? Show him, Mr. Rivers."

"Please. Not Mr. Rivers. I'm one of those agents who likes to work with local law enforcement as equals. Remember?"

Cliffie looked mightily pleased. Gary Cooper couldn't have delivered that last speech any better. "All right, go ahead and show the little prick your ID."

Which he did. I stared at the badge and the ID—Karl Rivers—and I still said, "Bullshit."

"Bullshit what?" Cliffie said.

"He's not an FBI man."

"Then where'd he get the ID?"

"You're starting to make me angry, Mr. McCain," Rivers said. "It's one thing to dislike me. It's another to question my credentials. Cliff here is the law in this town, and if my ID is good enough for him, I'd expect it to be good enough for you."

"He wants something of Conners, Sykes. He's up to something."

Cliffie said, "Of course he wants something of Conners. That's why he's here. The Agency's been trying to nail Conners for years. The fucking commie." Not lost on my ever-sensitive ear was the term "the Agency." Rivers had turned Cliffie into a junior FBI agent.

I knew there was no use arguing.

No use arguing at all.

"I hope I get a chance to buy you a drink sometime, Mr. McCain," Rivers said, as I walked out the door.

I HAD A couple of beers. One thing you can say about our little town is you've certainly got your choice of taverns. This particular one had a lot of songs from the forties on the jukebox. I like hearing them because they remind me of my mom and dad and that time right after the war when he was always bringing her little gifts, as if he had to court her all over again. And in a way, I suppose he did. He'd been gone for a long time and several of his friends had been killed and the dad who went wasn't exactly the dad who came back. He bought himself one good suit at J. C. Penney's and by God from 1946 to 1948 that suit was on his back three nights a week. Their favorite night out was on the dance boat *Moonglow*: a big dance floor with a small bar, a couple of rest rooms, and an upper deck where you could sit and watch the stars. It was a special night when you went on the *Moonglow*. Women wore corsages and men wore shoes so new they squeaked.

I was thinking about all this stuff because I didn't want to think about what I really *wanted* to think about. Namely how Rivers—and I doubted that was his name—had unmanned me. I don't mind losing a fight if I get in a few good punches. I've never been tough and I never will be. But I always make them pay for the privilege of beating the crap out of me. That way, they get the satisfaction of spilling some blood—mine—and I get the satisfaction of knowing I'm not a coward. So I had a couple of beers and thought about all the ways I could restore my manhood. I could drown him, burn him, hang him, dis-embowel him, suffocate him, run over him, throw him off a cliff, strangle him, stab him, shoot him, throw him in a snake pit, or make him listen to Liberace records. The trouble was, none of those alternatives seemed sufficiently nasty.

Most of the talk at the bar was about Conners's murder. You have to admire that in small towns. They give murder its due. In big cities, most murders get reported on page 17, if they get reported at all. But here we give them proper respect. A life has been taken. The entire town knows and honors it by talking about it. It is a seminal and communal experience for the most heinous of sins.

What surprised me was the goodwill these workingmen had for Conners. They didn't talk about his Jaguar or his philan-dering or his haughtiness. They talked about how hard he'd always stood for the common man. How he'd fought big busi-ness and how he'd seen to it that Iowa got drought relief and flood relief and medical care. And how his speeches stirred real passion at Memorial Day salutes to fallen soldiers. And how, when agribusiness started buying up small farms (in many cases, secretly arranging with city banks to pull loans that would force the small farms out of business), he had gone to the state legislature and whipped up the senators and represen-tatives who wouldn't accept the bribes the big agribusiness companies were offering. And the same with strikes. He was despised by businessmen and they were always hanging the "commie" charge around his neck. He might drive a Jaguar but he never forgot where he came from.

I'd planned on two beers. But I had three. And I felt better. Screw Rivers. No matter who he was or what he was after, he couldn't take Conners's legend away from him. I even started feeling sentimental about Conners, forgetting how much I'd despised him in some ways. Beer will do that to you. So will tales of a single man standing up against the power brokers.

I'D NEVER FELT embarrassed about seeing Mrs. Goldman before. We were good friends. Two or three times a week, she'd have me down for supper and we'd usually end up watching TV for a couple of hours on her new RCA console. It was a honey. We liked detective shows—the Warner Brothers ones especially, like "77 Sunset Strip."

But I felt pretty stupid tonight. This morning, drunk and all, I'd acted like a high school kid. Now I had a box of candy and six red roses in my hands as I came into the vestibule. I was about to tuck the chocolates under my arm so I could knock when the door opened up and there stood Mrs. Goldman. She had the figure of a much younger woman, and it never looked better than in jeans and a man's white button-down shirt. Es-pecially when she wore a cute little red bow on the right side of her head.

The spaghetti she was cooking reminded me that I hadn't eaten much today. She was one hell of a cook.

I started to say I was sorry but she stopped me. "You don't owe me an apology. You had a perfectly good reason for getting drunk. Your heart was broken." Then she smiled. "But the story doesn't end there."

"What story, Mrs. Goldman?"

"You and Pamela."

"Pamela?"

"Guess who's upstairs in your apartment?"

"You're kidding."

"About half an hour ago, she knocked on my door and asked if I'd let her in. Which was kind of funny because I thought I'd heard noises before that. Must be those mice you're always telling me about."

We have this running joke about my rent being lowered because of the mice—some of which, I claim from time to time, are the size of ponies.

"Anyway, she's waiting for you up there."

"I wonder what's wrong."

"Gosh, McCain. Look on the bright side. Maybe she decided you're the one she really loves."

I wouldn't allow myself to even think about it. *I'm the one she really loves after all.* Sure, and Dick Nixon has a portrait of Trotsky hanging in his office.

I pushed the candy and roses at her. "I am sorry about this morning."

She leaned forward and kissed me on the cheek, leaned far enough that her left breast brushed against me. Her breasts weren't particularly big but they sure were nice. "You're crazy, you know that? You can't afford things like this."

"My pleasure." I looked up the stairs leading to my second-floor apartment. "Wish me luck."

"Just remember." She laughed. "I love weddings."

"I'll be sure and mention that to her."

"Good luck. And thanks for the flowers."

The stairs. And Pamela waiting at the top of them. But why?

Not that she didn't drop by from time to time, she did. But not at this time of day. And she never stayed if I wasn't there. Could it be possible that Mrs. Goldman was right? That Pamela had finally perceived me as the truly wonderful guy I really am, superior in all ways (except for being able to beat the shit out of this phony FBI agent named Rivers) to all other beings of the male persuasion?

I wanted to dance up the stairs the way Donald O'Connor did in *Singin' in the Rain* and take her in my arms and kiss her as she'd never let me kiss her before.

But I was still aching from the run-in with Rivers and I needed to pee pretty bad and I had the beginnings of a headache. Other than that, I was a midwestern girl's dream man.

The door was unlocked. I pushed it inward. Darkness.

"What's that word they use in the movies for when somebody messes up your apartment while they're looking for something?" Pamela said from the couch.

"You mean tossed?"

"Right. Tossed. That's what somebody did to your apartment."

"Aw, shit."

"But don't turn on the light, OK? I need to talk to you and I can't do it if the lights're on. And I owe you about a third of a bottle of bourbon."

"That's a lot for you."

She giggled. Only then did I realize she was bombed. "And for you. You can't hold your liquor any better than I can." Then she said, "I shouldn't be laughing."

"Why not?"

"Have a drink with me first."

You have to appreciate how strange this all was. Her being let into my apartment. Her drinking my bourbon. Her getting drunk. I'd never seen her even tight before. Women who wear those cute little white gloves everywhere they go shouldn't be allowed to get drunk. It's against their charter.

I stumbled a couple times getting myself a glass, and I tripped getting back to the couch and the bottle. By then, my eyes had adjusted to the darkness. Pale moonlight gave a ghostly glow to her white slip. And that's all she appeared to be wearing.

She said, "I want you to make love to me."

"What?"

"You heard me."

"Pamela, are you all right?"

"All these years you've been begging me to make love and now I throw myself at you and you say no?"

"I'm not saying no, Pamela. I'm just trying to figure out what's going on here."

"I'm a home wrecker, that's what's going on here."

"You're not a home wrecker."

"Oh, yes, I am. Just like Barbara Stanwyck."

"I thought it was Alexis Smith."

"It *was* Alexis Smith. But I saw another movie last night. Barbara Stanwyck was an even bigger home wrecker than Alexis Smith." Then: "Pour yourself a drink."

I poured myself a drink.

"Do you have the things?"

"Things?"

"You know, Trojans."

"Pamela, we really should talk first."

"All these years, McCain, all these years. And you finally get your chance and you say no. . . . Oh, God."

"What?"

"I'm going to be sick."

"I'll help you."

"No! I don't want you to see me sick, for God's sake. That's what'd come to your mind every time you saw me."

"No, it wouldn't. I've helped lots of people puke."

"That isn't something I'd brag about."

She barely made it. She tripped too, over stuff that had been strewn across the floor by an intruder. He'd even left a faint stench behind. Honoring my commitment to live in a cave, I found a flashlight in my kitchenette drawer (don't you love that word, kitchenette?) and started tallying up the damage. Tender and loving he hadn't been. At least the cats were okay. I found them cowering under the bed. He went through drawers, firing everything back over his shoulder. He went in, around, and through all the furniture. And he had no hesitation about dumping out my sugar and flour, looking for whatever hidden treasure drove him onward.

As for Pamela, she was real serious about me not participating in her vomiting. She ran both faucets and the shower, which blocked out all other sounds. She was in there a good twenty minutes, during which time I picked up the phone and called the Judge.

She had one of her midweek cocktail parties going, mostly other judges and lawyers from Cedar Rapids and Iowa City. Men of the Republican species, mostly. Her man Abernathy took my call. "At the moment, she's showing Judge Reinhold how to cha-cha."

"Tell her it's important."

"Between you and me, I think she has a crush on Judge Reinhold."

"Ah. How sweet. Interrupt her anyway."

She came on the line a few minutes later. "McCain, I realize that you're not acquainted with the folkways of civilized people, but seven-thirty-five in the evening is a vulgar time to be interrupting." She was flying high on brandy and the charms of Judge Reinhold, whoever he might be.

"I need you to call your friend J. Edgar and confirm an agent of his."

"And this can't wait till tomorrow?"

"You're in court from eight on. He'll be busy and you'll be busy and it'll be another day before this guy gets identified."

She sighed. "All right." I could hear loud cha-cha music in the background. "Give me the man's name."

I gave her Rivers's full name. I also gave her a description. The music continued to blare. I imagined all those judges doing the cha-cha in their black robes.

"I'll call him first thing in the morning."

I said, "So how're you and Judge Reinhold getting along?"

"That damned Abernathy. He's worse than Louella Parsons. Gossip gossip gossip. We're just good friends. We belong to the same riding club here and the same yachting club in Florida. Now, is there anything else your dirty little mind would like to know?"

PAMELA WAS STILL in the john. I turned on the TV. Two cowboy shows and a detective show. I turned it off. Couldn't concentrate on anything except the prospect of making love.

Since fourth grade I'd loved her. Emotionally I loved her, spiritually I loved her, sexually I loved her. And here was my chance—so why hadn't I just dragged her right across my messy floor into my messy bed?

She came out a very different girl than she'd gone in. Wore a button-down shirt of mine. Long golden hair now pulled back into a chignon. Exuding sobriety. I could tell all this even in the darkness. "You have a cigarette? I ran out."

"Sure." I gave her a cigarette.

"Mind if I make some coffee?"

"Not at all. But I've just got instant."

"That's fine." She put on the teakettle. Made herself a cup, silent all the while. Went back and sat down on the couch.

"You figured it out yet?" she said.

"Figured what out yet?"

"Why I'm here?"

"I guess not."

She sighed and took another sip of coffee. Picked up another Lucky from my pack. I extended my Zippo lighter.

She sat back against the couch, closed her eyes, smoked her cigarette. The shirttails didn't extend far down her legs. I could see her panties. Lust was getting the best of me.

"He went home and told his wife about me and then *she* told *him* about an affair *she'd* been having, and then they both realized what terrible people they'd been as spouses and as parents. So practically in the middle of the night, they went to see their pastor—you know that Episcopalian, Reverend Loughgren—and they told him everything and he blessed them and now they're happily married again. My reputation is zilch in this town now. Zilch. And I come from a good family, too."

No tears. No dramatics. She sort of laid it all out, in fact. "So what do I do? I come over here and sit around practically naked and offer myself to you. Now that makes a lot of sense, doesn't it? Thanks for not taking me up on it. You're a real gentleman. It wouldn't have meant anything to me, and I know you don't want it that way."

"Well," I said. "Well, well, well."

"I mean, I just wanted to hurt him. But I see now that if I'd gone to bed with you, I'd just have ended up hurting myself."

I think I probably threw in several more "well, well, well's" somewhere along the way. But I was speaking on automatic pilot. Because if I'd ever needed the cold slap of confirmation, she'd just given it to me. The slap that said she didn't love me romantically and never would.

Then she said, "You know what I'd like to do, though?"

"What?"

"Could we just lie down and you just hold me?"

God, was she hard to figure out.

"I mean, we'd keep our clothes on and everything."

"Oh." It was going to be like high school again, you lying beside her and every time you brush against her—your body just one giant erection—she says, in the voice of a much put-upon saint, "Please, McCain, I thought we were just going to lie here and not do anything."

"I know it's a lot to ask and it's really unfair—because we won't be doing anything or anything—but I really just need to be held. You ever get like that? Where you just ache to have somebody hold you like you're a little kid?"

"Nah," I lied, "I never felt like that."

"I'm really down, McCain. Please just be near me."

SHE CRIED, WEPT, sobbed, shrieked, gasped, wailed, moaned, and once even screamed. And I'm not using a thesaurus here, either.

I had a lot of what you call mixed emotions—which usually means, in my experience, that you don't much care for what someone is doing. I guess I was jealous, mostly. It sure would be nice if she cared enough about *me* to do any of the things listed above. On the other hand, when I was being more rational about it, I saw we were in the same fix. Stu, the selfish prick, had broken her heart and she had broken mine.

About half an hour after we stretched out on the bed, she went to sleep. There were two things wrong with this by my calculations. One was that my arm was under her head and was already numb. The other was that, because of the angle of my useless arm, I was pressed against her backside and every time she squirmed even a little bit—well, I'll let you imagine the rest for yourself.

It happened about an hour into our little emotional sojourn on the bed. I was dozing off; my arm by now had atrophied. My dad had a good saw. We could save hospital money and just do the amputation ourselves. It'd be like pruning a tree.

I was dozing and not aware and—

And then she was facing me and kissing me, and when I tried to say something she inserted her tongue in my mouth to shut me up. And then a moment of terror. All those years I'd loved her so much and wanted her so badly, what if, in the moment when it was about to happen, I couldn't—

As she started to strip away the shirt she was wearing, I realized that certain parts of my body weren't responding the way they should. Here, just twenty minutes ago I couldn't get the damned thing to behave itself, and now—

But then we were kissing again and her silken fingers moved down my stomach. A brief touch was all it took and then— thank God—I was ready.

"WELL," SHE SAID afterward, in the darkness. "Was it worth the wait?"

I felt so many different things—exultation, simple love, complex love, and a terrible fear that now I'd never get over her; I'd actually slept with her and was hooked for life, like poor old shambling Lon Chaney Jr. in all those werewolf movies— that I wasn't quite sure what to say. But I knew what she *wanted* me to say, so I said it. "God, are you kidding. It was wonderful."

"I taste all right?"

"You tasted fine."

"I really try to keep myself clean. Some girls I know don't even try."

"You taste great."

She snuggled close to me beneath the covers. It would have been a completely heady moment except for the fact that I really *really* needed to empty ye olde bladder. "You're a very good lover, McCain."

"Thanks."

"You make sure the girl's having a good time. Stu doesn't care at all. Very selfish."

"He looks like the kind."

"He does?"

"I was joking."

"Oh."

I just kept thinking about how badly I needed to pee. But I also kept thinking that this might be my one and only night with Pamela. Ever. So I could hardly get up and walk to the john and ruin the moment, could I?

"He also can't last very long."

She was doing what we all do when we've been hurt. Diminish the person who has hurt us. By the end of the night, Stu would be this guy with skin like alligator hide and connections to a satanic cult.

"Plus his breath—whew. It's pretty rank."

"He sounds ducky."

"Your breath is excellent, McCain."

"Excellent," I said. "Now there's a nice word for breath. The Excellent Breath Award goes to Sam McCain. Maybe Connie Francis could present it to me on *Bandstand* some afternoon."

"Really. It is. And I'm not just saying that."

We lay there for a time, silently. She was thinking of him

and I was thinking of her. And then the cats hit the bed and then we were all tangled up together: the beautiful Pamela, Tasha, Crystal, and Tess. There was a plethora of new scents and sounds for them to take in. Tasha is particularly responsive to voices and Pamela has a nice one, throaty but refined. Tess presented me with a pretty good view of her butt several times. Crystal made sure my chin was clean, and Tasha thoughtfully lay on my head in case I was getting cold.

Pamela said, "You ever wish the night would never end?"

"Sometimes."

"This is one of those nights. I'd like to stay right here in this bed with you and your cats forever. Never be dawn again. It feels so safe here."

Translate to *I don't have to deal with my feelings for Stu tonight; I can just float along in this bed. It's a beautiful escape.* I knew that's what she was feeling because it's what *I* was feeling too. If we could just stay here forever—and if this was the final night, never to be daylight again—how simple and lucky my life would be. Especially if I got to go to the bathroom soon.

"And it's not like I don't have feelings for you," she said.

This was the part I wasn't going to like. You know, where she tried to rationalize herself out of love with Stu and into love with me. It was sort of like trying hard to fall in love with your hamster.

"And it's not like you're not a lot of fun.

"And it's not like you're ugly or anything.

"And it's not like you don't have a future.

"And it's not like you wouldn't be a good provider and a wonderful father.

"And it's not like you'd ever cheat on me or start drinking or beat me or anything."

And then she fell to crying again because she was so miserable at the prospect of marrying me, she couldn't face it.

I decided that this was a good time to get up and take my whizz. I'd pretty much used up all my sobbing patter anyway. *There there now; hey, hey, c'mon, you'll feel a lot better in the morning; hey, this isn't like you, you're a fighter; you don't give up just because Stu decided to go back to his wife.*

I had just set foot on the floor when the phone rang. She went right on crying and the cats were glad to see me get up and go. More room for them to stretch out.

I picked up the phone and this voice said hello and my first reaction—and I'm serious—was that it was a joke. I'll just give you the dialogue and stand back out of the way.

"Hello."

"McCain?"

"Yes."

"McCain, this is Stu Grant. I know this is a little awkward but—is Pamela there?"

"Pamela?"

"Yes. I—need to talk to her."

"Is that for me?"

"Just a second, Stu. Yeah, it's for you."

"Did you say 'Stu'? My God, is that Stu on the phone?"

"I know this is awkward for you, McCain. I really appreciate you putting her on the line."

"Oh, God, please bring the phone over here. I can't believe he'd call here."

"Just a second, Stu."

That's how it started. She wrapped the sheet around her, very primlike, and sat on the edge of the bed, and I handed her the phone. Then she pointed to the nightstand and my cigarettes. I lighted a Lucky for her. Then she said, "Stu, just a minute." Then, "Thanks very much, McCain. I really appreciate this." Which meant, Get the hell out of here, McCain, so I can talk in private. It was one of those moments when I wish my folks hadn't raised me to be so polite. I mean, I should've told both of them where to go. But if you're raised to be polite, you can't quite get the words out, break the social contract that way. "Really appreciate this," she said again, to scoot me on my way.

Talk about the world's most appreciating couple. He appreciated. She appreciated. It was a real orgy of appreciation all the way around.

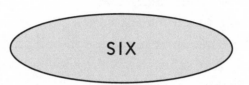

SIX

Well, if nothing else, I finally got to take my pee.

I sort of cleaned up, too. This gave me an excuse to run the water so it wouldn't seem as if I was trying to eavesdrop. Something was up, that was for sure, him calling here this way.

I had a shirt and some jeans hanging in the john closet. After I shaved and brushed my teeth and combed my hair, I put them on and slid my feet into my old penny loafers. I bought them in 1948 in the boys' department at Adams' Department Store downtown. And for doing so, I got a cellophane envelope containing six Batman comic books. You can't get bargains like that anymore. I was fourteen at the time and the shoes still fit eleven years later. That should tell you something about my size.

When I turned the water off and the light out, I heard something terrifying. The sound of Pamela throwing her clothes on so she could leave me.

I cleared my throat and strolled out into the moonlight-traced apartment.

She was dressed. Standing in the middle of the floor, wobbling around on one foot so she could pull on her other shoe.

"Oh, God, McCain. It's all so crazy."

Yeah, I thought, I'll bet it is.

"You know what he said?"

She was going to tell me anyway.

"He's picking me up at my house in half an hour. I'm supposed to pack two suitcases. We're moving to Chicago. Tonight! He said things'd just be too hard for us here. The way people would put us down and everything. He said we need a fresh start. He's going to marry me, McCain! He's going to marry me!"

Then she was throwing her arms around me and hugging me and sort of leading us in a native dance of joy and celebration. And I hated her and I loved her and I wanted her again and I hated her and I loved her. But I couldn't blame her exactly, either. She'd waited for him just about as long as I'd waited for her. It was like dying standing there; my whole life with her came tumbling back. The walks home to the Knolls in autumn. Seeing her in her first two-piece at the public swimming pool. Holding hands as we ice skated in the winter. All the corny cards and sappy letters I'd sent her. And now it was all done, all over.

Then, at last, she was tender. "Tonight'll be our little secret, McCain. And I'll never forget it. You were so sweet and gentle with me. You're going to make somebody a great little husband, you really are."

We were back to the World's Most Boring Husband. With the qualifying "little" thrown in.

Her last kiss was passionate and tender and made me ready to go again. But to no avail. She was at the door saying, "Boy, you really should find out what that smell is. I think your intruder left something behind."

*   *   *

I TURNED ON the lights. I figured I couldn't feel any worse. He/she/they had done a good job as tossing standards go. The kitchen floor was covered with mounds of flour, sugar, coffee, salt. That's about as far as I got. I didn't want to see any more of the mess. Not right now. I took what was left of the whiskey and sat in the armchair and drank and smoked and thought up all the neat things I'd say to Pamela and Stu Grant the next time I saw them. Boy, would they be sorry they'd taken advantage of my good nature. And then there was the ultimate daydream: it's midnight on a rainy evening and there's a knock on my back door and there stands Pamela, drenched and sobbing. As soon as she sees me, she throws her arms around me and says, "I ran all the way back from Chicago! I love you, McCain, I love you!" I know it's corny, but you know how it is when you fantasize. When I was little, I used to pretend I was Batman, so I guess my fantasies have gotten a little more realistic. Except for that running all the way from Chicago bit, at least.

My fantasies ran out just about the same time the whiskey did. And I was down to three cigarettes. I was starting to get cold.

And that's when the smell really started getting to me. It was pretty awful, but I'd been in so much turmoil. Given everything else that was going on, a smell wasn't much to worry about.

I hadn't checked any of the closets. I took the flashlight from next to the bedroom and went looking for the source of the stench.

If you've read more than three detective novels, you've probably already figured out what I was about to discover. It was in the second closet I looked in. In the back. Under a pile of clothes.

The more clothes I pulled off, the worse the smell got.

And then, there he was.

Karl Rivers. Or whatever his name really was. Dead.

From what I could see, somebody had hit him pretty hard with something pretty heavy on the side of the head. A blunt instrument, as Agatha Christie would describe it.

The smell was coming from his bowels and his blood. He wore the same gray Brooks Brothers suit he'd had on back at the college. His eyes were closed. His fingers were claws.

"Aw, shit," I said.

There was no way around it. I would have to pick up the phone and call Cliffie Sykes Jr.

PART II

SEVEN

SO THERE YOU ARE," Cliffie said to me, forty-three and a half minutes later, in the midst of the melee that was my apartment.

"So there I am," I said.

"Standing in the doorway of your apartment."

"Standing in the doorway of my apartment."

"And you see that your place has been tossed."

We all must've gone to the same movies. Everybody knew what *tossed* meant.

"And I see that the place has been tossed."

"And you didn't think there might be a dead guy in your apartment?"

"Why would I think there's a dead guy in my apartment?"

"A dead—may I remind you?—FBI man."

"Pamela was here and we had some things to talk about."

"So you didn't think there might be a dead guy in the closet?"

"No. I didn't think there might be a blue buffalo in my closet, either. I told you, Pamela and I had personal things to discuss."

"What things?"

"Personal things. Things that don't have anything to do with this."

"I'll be the judge of that."

I sighed. "She and a friend were having some troubles. She needed to talk about it."

"What friend?"

"What difference does it make what friend? Just a friend is all."

"Male or female?"

"God, Sykes, what's the difference?"

Two things interrupted our little verbal dance. Deputy Henry Regennitter came pounding up the back steps shouting—this is now around 1 A.M. and people are trying to sleep: all those, anyway, not encircling the emergency vehicles downstairs— and the phone rang.

I leapt for the phone, suspecting who it might be. Cliffie probably wouldn't let me talk to her if he got it.

"No such agent," Esme Anne Whitney said to me, in a sleepy, brandied voice. "I was going to call Edgar in the morning and ask him to check it out for me. But Clyde—and this is between us—is a much nicer guy when you wake him up in the middle of the night." I suppose I could've asked her how she would have come to know that particular fact, but all I said, ever the gentleman, was, "Anything else?"

Deputy Regennitter had found something, and Cliffie and Deputy Roger Weed were examining it carefully—i.e., handing it back and forth and getting their fingerprints all over it. I'm smarter than that. After I got my law degree and realized I couldn't support myself in Black River Falls as an attorney—at least not right out of the chute—I took Judge Whitney's advice and went back to the U of Iowa and took several criminology courses and got my private investigator's license. And one of the first things they teach you in private eye school—right after you learn about which kind of trench coat to buy and all the variations on the private eye's secret handshake—is to be very careful how you handle evidence. It's all right to soak it, jump up and down on it, or even lick it if you're so inclined, but they do urge one never to muck it up with one's own fingerprints if at all possible. Cliffie must not have been in class that day.

"Oh, yes," the Judge said, very enthused now. "One other bit of tantalizing information. Rivers—his real name was Andrew Wylie—was let go from the Agency because of his activities with some far-right organizations. The Agency was so concerned about him they kept track of him after he left Washington. He went to work for an outfit called America First. They've been active in stirring up trouble with small-town school boards: getting teachers fired, taking certain books out of school libraries, starting whispering campaigns about certain prominent citizens. And guess who the outfit's representative in Black River Falls is? And the man Rivers contacted when he got here three days ago? Jeff Cronin."

"McCain, who the hell you talking to?" Cliffie said.

"I'd better go," I said to the Judge. "And you know, sometimes you almost sound like a liberal."

"Good Lord, that's the vilest thing anybody's ever said to me." She hung up.

Cliffie came over, bearing gifts.

"Regennitter found this in the garage," Cliffie said, proudly pushing it toward me. "The killer must've tossed it there when he was making his getaway." He made it sound as if we were in a Hopalong Cassidy movie.

There wasn't much doubt it had been used as a weapon. There was relatively fresh blood, small tufts of hair, and the mucus-like gray matter of the human brain.

"It's mine," I said.

Cliffie grinned. "You like Pat Boone? I thought you only liked coon music—Chuck Berry and that crowd."

"Always the poet, aren't you, Cliffie?"

"Don't call me Cliffie."

"Then don't call people coons. You ever heard of the civil rights movement?"

Cliffie smirked at Deputy Roger Weed. "Oh, I heard of it, all right. I figure Martin Luther King's got about six months before somebody starts usin' him for target practice."

Hopeless.

"The bust is mine, Cliffie."

"Bust?"

"That's what it's called: a bust." A bust of Pat Boone, with *God Bless Rock-and-Roll* inscribed along the bottom. Weighed about three pounds. Mary Travers, the girl I probably would've married if it hadn't been for Pamela, bought it for me as a joke, knowing how much I hated Pat Boone. I explained this to Cliffie.

"Maybe you used this yourself tonight."

"I didn't."

"You prove it?"

"Yes. Doc Novotny can give you a pretty good approximation of the time he was killed. I wasn't here at the time." Then I said, "And by the way, he wasn't an FBI agent."

"Bullshit. He showed me his ID."

"Fake." I explained who he'd really been. I told him about America First. "I bet I can tell you who introduced you to him, too."

"Who?"

"Jeff Cronin."

As we talked, new people kept coming into my apartment, front and back. Cliffie had called in some help from Cedar Rapids. A photographer, a man dusting for prints, a man making notes on where the body had been, a man matching two footprints to the soles of the dead man's shoes. A while back, Cliffie's incompetence had messed up an otherwise open-and-shut case for the local county attorney. The county attorney happened to be his first cousin. He went to Cliffie's old man and told him how everybody looked bad when Cliffie made mistakes like this and how if he wanted to leave Cliffie as police chief, for God's sake get him some good help when it was needed. So Cliffie Sr. called some friends of his, and Cedar Rapids agreed to lend a hand. They were pros and would save Cliffie from being Cliffie. Unless he got his hands on the evidence first, as he did with the bust of Pat Boone.

Cliffie looked unhappy. He was starting to put it together. I decided to make him unhappier.

"So he lied to you."

"Who lied to me?" Cliffie said.

"Your good friend Jeff Cronin. At least he did if he told you Rivers—and that wasn't his real name, by the way—was FBI. He got kicked out a year ago."

"Kicked out?"

"You better talk to your buddy Cronin."

"Wouldn't lie to me."

"No? Well, somebody did. Unless you were lying to me when you introduced him as FBI."

"You saw the badge."

"Yeah, for about a second and a half I saw the badge."

"Wouldn't bullshit me like that." He looked stunned, as if he'd just discovered that the world wasn't flat after all. "She alibi you on all this stuff?"

"Pamela?"

"Yeah."

"She would if she wasn't headed to Chicago."

"What's she going to Chicago for this time of night?"

"Start her new life there with Stu Grant."

He smirked. "Yeah, sure. Then next week she's gonna sing on Ed Sullivan."

"I'm serious. They've been seeing each other on the sly for a long time now."

"My ass, McCain. I'm the frigging law here. Anybody's having an affair, Cliff Sykes, Junior knows about it."

"Wait till morning," I said. "It'll be all over town by then."

"Stu Grant? He's gonna run for governor. He'd never do anything like that. Besides, he's a Methodist."

I wasn't quite sure what that last bit meant exactly, but as it turned out I didn't have time to find out.

A new man came in just then. Wore a suit, looked smart and official. Saw the blood all over the bust of Pat Boone that Deputies Weed and Regennitter were handing back and forth. "I actually like some of his songs," Regennitter was saying. "I mean, I don't know why people're always making fun of him."

The new man said, "Making fun of who?"

"Pat Boone."

"That, I take it, is blood," the new man said.

"Yeah," Weed said, "and that sticky shit is brain goop."

The new man said, "This is the murder weapon?"

"We're pretty sure it is," Regennitter said.

"And you're handling it like this?" the new man said, sounding a note of utter disbelief.

"Yeah," Weed said. "Why?"

The new man came over to Cliffie and introduced himself as a member of the State Bureau of Investigation. "Judge Whitney called my boss. He asked me to drive over here on her word."

"Judge Whitney?" Cliffie said, profoundly aggrieved. "She don't have no say who gets asked into a case like this."

The new man lowered his voice and nodded his head back toward Weed and Regennitter. "Those two men of yours."

"Yeah?" Cliffie said. "What about 'em?"

"I strongly suspect," the new man said, "that they're idiots."

EIGHT

I got to sleep around two-thirty. Mrs. Goldman was nice enough to let me use her guest room, while Cliffie was forced to establish my apartment as a crime scene. She was even nice enough to make breakfast for me when I woke up around nine. She said the Judge had called but said to let me sleep in. Then I was to head straight to her chambers.

Mrs. Mannering, a widow who usually works upstairs in the county clerk's office, was sitting in Pamela's chair when I got there. The reception area was otherwise empty.

"Could you cover me later for a half-hour lunch, McCain?" she said.

"Sure, if you'll show me how to use that phone contraption." The Judge had four lines.

I noticed a tiny tic in the corner of her eye socket.

"I'm going to need my nerve pills," she said. She was a sweet-faced woman with a fondness for pies—her photo was in the paper every year for winning first place at the county fair for her blueberry pie—and Barbara Cartland novels. Any time she had a free moment, her button nose was pushed deep into a paperback.

She leaned forward and whispered. "Do you know Judge Whitney yells?"

"I've heard rumors."

"And that she sips brandy all the time?"

"Another rumor."

"And smokes those terrible French cigarettes? I can't even pronounce the name."

I nodded. "We should just be thankful she doesn't chew tobacco."

She giggled at the image of Esme Anne Whitney biting off a chunk of Red Man.

"Well, wish me luck."

Her tic took a violent turn. "I just need to get some of my nerve pills; then I'll be all right. I just hope I don't get transferred down here permanently."

THE DESIGNER ATTIRE today was rather simple, something Hepburn—in this case, Audrey—might have worn: simple but very feminine white blouse, fitted blue skirt, blue stockings, blue flats. The matching jacket was on the coat stand.

She had parked her prim well-bred can on the edge of her always-clean desk. She had a snifter of brandy, and a Gauloise burning in the ashtray.

"Mrs. Mannering fears for her life," I said.

"Good," she said. "Nothing motivates people like terror. My father was a colonel in the First World War and told me all about it."

"I'm assuming he fought on our side."

"Very funny, McCain." Then, lifting both brandy snifter and

cigarette, she said, "So what, pray God, is going on in this town?"

I started to open my mouth but she stopped me.

"You probably aren't aware of it, but my birthday is coming up and several of my closest friends are flying out to celebrate it with me. I know you think I'm to the right of Hitler in my politics, but believe it or not I regard all this red-baiting stuff as very low-class. It's how the Nazis took over Germany; they toppled the elite by accusing them of treason. And that's what's going on here now. At tonight's school board meeting, someone is going to try and get a teacher removed. My God, it'll make national news! We'll look like a bunch of cretins!"

I didn't want to correct her history and explain that treason charges weren't *exactly* how the Nazis came to power, but she was close enough so I let it slide. I'd tried only once before to correct the Judge. It is a day not even electroshock therapy could help me forget.

"For the sake of the town—before we all look like a bunch of fanatics—please find out what's going on and stop it. Even my conservative friends will think we've lost our minds."

"That's what I've been trying to do ever since Richard Conners got killed. But things came—"

She held up her hand for silence. "I of course know what you mean by 'things.' My God, how could this have been going on without my knowing it?"

"That's what Cliffie said."

"You knew?"

"Of course."

"And you didn't tell me? Stu Grant's wife and I are on the library board together. Do you know how it's going to look when I see her tomorrow? As if I've known all along what was going on but let Pamela work here anyway. My God, I didn't think you and she were—well, you know, McCain, nothing personal—on the same social plane. But I would've preferred her running off with you!"

"Thanks."

"Oh, don't go and get all sensitive on me. You know what I'm saying."

"Well," I said, "I'm not really all that thrilled about it either."

She looked at me, and for just an infinitesimal moment I saw a flash of sympathy in her gaze. "No, I don't suppose you are, are you?" Then: "If I was one of those hugging sorts of people, I'd probably give you a hug now and tell you to buck up or whatever the Brits say."

I stood up. "That's all right. I've had a lot of hugs lately and they haven't seemed to do me much good."

"Then you'll get right on it?"

"Right away."

When I reached the door, she said, "And from now on, if something's going on in my office that I should know about, McCain, I expect you to tell me."

"Well," I said, "in that case, I think there's something going on between Mrs. Mannering and the mailman."

"Very funny," she said, taking a deep drink of her brandy. "Very, very funny."

I STOPPED BY the office to look at the mail and see if there were any checks. There weren't. The Judge paid me well enough that I never had to worry about making the rent or buying food, but it would have been nice to know that my legal clients thought enough of my services to pay me every now and then.

Mom called, just as I was leaving, to remind me of what day

it was, and I instantly felt like hell for not remembering. So much had happened, the significance of this particular day had been lost to me.

I WAS ACTUALLY being followed. I wanted to call somebody and tell them. *You know how in detective movies, somebody is always following our guy in a car? Well, somebody's following me in a car right now. A blue 1954 Nash. Staying about a quarter block behind me. Pretty cool, huh?*

The stuff you'd think they'd cover in instructing you how to get your private investigator's license, they never do. How to get rid of unwanted blondes who keep breaking into your office and stripping. How to store all those empty fifths of Jim Beam. And how to get the gum off your soles after tailing somebody all day. Never a word about *any* of that practical stuff. Or about how to lose a car that's following you.

THERE ARE A couple of ways you can get to the Connerses' manor house on the other side of the river. The most convenient and popular way is to drive across the Lyman bridge and then up into the hills on gravel roads. This time of year, the trip is spellbinding, the leaves and all. You even get a chance to see some of the Indian mounds constructed as grave sites four or five hundred years ago. When you're in seventh grade, they pile you into an old yellow school bus and take you on a tour of these hills. A lot of Indian lore here, and a lot of it sad. Still, there isn't a race on earth that can claim sainthood. Every tribe has its victims and victimizers. The same with people who think things only get worse. I remember arguing with somebody once about how only our age had stooped to biological warfare. I reminded him that in the mid-1300s the Tartars used to throw corpses of Black Death victims at their enemies. A jolly bunch, we humans.

The other way to reach the manor house is by water. Ernie Paul runs a combination grocery, bait, and boat rental place next to a small dock. Personally, I don't care to buy food while my nostrils are clogged with the stench of live bait, but Ernie does well for himself. The interior of his store is covered with photos of his two years in Korea, which is where he lost his right eye. The black eyepatch has a yellow University of Iowa football logo on it. It matches the yellow-and-black Hawkeye suspenders he always wears.

We went down to the river, where he keeps three wooden rowboats during the day. I carried the oars he'd handed me. We got the boat into the water and he said, "They know you're comin'?"

"Just thought I'd drop in."

He shook his angular graying head. "They don't like it when you surprise them. I took a birthday cake out to old Dorothy a couple of years ago. You know, a surprise for the old gal. I thought the bastards was gonna lynch me." Then he laughed. "But you sneak up real nice and quiet, you might get a gander of Chris Tomlin sunbathin' nude up on the bluff there."

"Chris Tomlin?" Though I found her sexual in a quiet way, there was something so earnestly grad school about her, I couldn't imagine her lying outside in the buff.

"She's a hot number, the way I hear it."

That's another thing about Ernie, he's a gossip. If the candy machine guy was reliable only 50 percent of the time, Ernie is reliable less than that. He once tried to tell me that our mayor—a Sykes-clan cousin of advanced age who has suffered two heart attacks and is known to have hemorrhoids so bad he'll start stamping his feet and jerking up and down in his chair right in the middle of a city council meeting—was having an affair with a "high yella" woman in Cedar Rapids. Sure, Ernie.

I got in the boat.

"Water's rough today, McCain. Be careful."

I nodded. He gave me a good shove.

I needed the fresh air. The water lapped blue and wide between the steep cliffs topped by birches and oaks and hardwoods, their leaves igniting in blazing yellows and umbers and mauve. Downriver you could see fishermen standing in their motorboats, casting. Rowing felt good; the Iowa air purified me. Even my hangover began to recede.

Steps had been built into the side of the clay-and-shale hillside. I tied the boat and climbed them.

The house resembled a movie set, one of those giant Tudors where Greer Garson and Ronald Coleman always lived, the exterior walls of brick and native stone acrawl with venerable tangles of vine, two soaring chimneys sending gray smoke into the autumnal blue sky to deflect the chill, mullioned windows and massive doors like the accoutrements of medieval castles. To the right of the Tudor, and set far back next to woods beyond the clearing, was a small house of the same brick and stone. A girl of four or five rode a red tricycle up and down the empty asphalt drive, ringing a handlebar bell as pure and clear as her thoughts.

I heard voices out back and walked around the massive house. Someday, I'd have one just like this. A wife and two kids and my red ragtop. And maybe write a mystery or two. And pose for photos in houndstooth jackets with briar pipes in my teeth and cats in my arms like Raymond Chandler.

Dana Conners was raking leaves into a wheelbarrow next to an old black Ford panel truck with the passenger door stove in. Near her, next to a garden shed, Dorothy was picking up handfuls of leaves from another wheelbarrow and putting them into a large open incinerator. She seemed to be taking no chances. She squirted some kind of fire starter on them, tossed in a match, and the whole thing went *whoosh!*, like an effect in a movie.

"She doesn't take any chances, does she?" I said.

"Dorothy? She loves to burn stuff. If I didn't know better, I'd say she was a pyromaniac."

Just then, the little girl on the tricycle rang her bell again. I smiled in her direction.

"She's sweet, isn't she?" Dana said. She wore a tan turtle-neck and a Western belt, jeans, and cordovan Western boots. Lissome as always but still a bit dazed-seeming.

"She sure is. Hope I have one just like her someday."

She looked at me carefully. "You're a sentimental man."

"I suppose."

"Richard was, too. But he didn't want people to know. Thought it would damage his reputation as a negotiator." Her blue eyes shone abruptly with tears; her model's body bent oddly, as if wounded in some way. "I loved him, McCain. Probably more than I should have."

I wasn't sure what that meant, but it didn't seem appropriate to question her about it.

Dorothy came over, taking off her brown cotton work gloves. Man's blue work shirt, dark glasses, wrinkled pair of chinos with patches of apple-green paint on them. Apple-green paint on the worn penny loafers, too. "Cliffie's been out here twice. He's a fool. He seems to think that either Dana or I killed Richard. He even asked us for alibis."

"And you had one?" I said.

"God," Dorothy said. "You too?"

"Of course we had one," Dana snapped. "We were together, in fact—shopping. We drove into town together."

"Why not ride with Richard?"

"Because," Dana said, "he didn't have an appointment till half an hour later."

"There," Dorothy snapped. "Are you satisfied?"

"Believe it or not, Dorothy," I said, "Cliffie had every right to ask you that question."

"He was my son."

"Murder among family members isn't unheard of."

"I thought you were smarter than that, McCain," she said. She made a face, stepped away, and went back to the incinerator.

"The doctor gave her a sedative," Dana said. "I don't think it's working very well. She's agitated all the time." She paused. "It's ridiculous to think she did it."

"Yes," I said. "It probably is. But you have to ask."

"I've never heard you defend that moron before."

"Well, when he's right, he's right."

She knew I was studying her. "And it's just as ridiculous to think that *I* killed him."

"Had you been getting along?"

"Very well, for your information." Then: "Do you know what this feels like? Dorothy is mourning a son and I'm mourning a husband, and here you are asking if one of us killed him. We're trying to arrange things for his funeral and that's not fun at all."

"Somebody murdered him."

"So the Judge wants to beat Cliffie to the punch as usual, is that it? Show that her boy McCain is smarter than Sykes's boy Cliffie and can solve the murder faster. God, I wish she'd grow up!"

I said, "You're not interested in who killed him?"

Some of the anger drained from her face. She leaned on the handle of the rake she'd been using. "That's the funny thing. I do and I don't. I mean, on the one hand, sure I want to see who did it brought to justice. But on the other hand, what difference will it make? Richard will still be dead. Dorothy and I will still be alone."

Chris Tomlin appeared with a big collie in tow. They went over to the little girl on the tricycle. The golden dog jumped up playfully on the girl and began licking her. The girl giggled and screamed at the same time; Chris, laughing, pulled the dog off.

"I wonder what Bill Tomlin will do," I said.

"I wonder the same thing. He leached off Richard all his life."

"That seems a little harsh. Richard always said he couldn't have accomplished anything without Bill helping him."

"Richard was a very generous man. He overpraised everybody, and I include myself. And Bill never had the good sense to be appreciative. They've been fighting a lot lately. Bill demanded co-author credit on the biography. Not 'as told to' but full co-author credit."

"They argued?"

She smiled coldly. "I seem to have handed you another suspect, haven't I?"

"Did you ever see the man named Rivers up here?"

"No," she said. "But I've given that some thought."

"What kind of thought?"

"What if they were in cahoots."

"Rivers and Bill?"

"Yes. What if Bill was going to tell Rivers some secrets about Richard, secrets Rivers and his people could use to discredit him when the book came out."

She wouldn't make a bad detective. But then why, if you followed her implication far enough, would Bill have killed

Rivers? "I'll think about that. Now I'd like to talk to Chris—Mrs. Tomlin."

"You and every other man in this town."

This time I inquired about her enigmatic statement. "That mean anything in particular?"

"It means what it means," she said, pulling on her own brown cotton work gloves. "Maybe she'll make you a drink and you can have a nice long discussion about Aristotle."

Her bitterness was startling. You wouldn't think a woman with her looks and style would ever have anything to be bitter about.

"I take it you don't get along?"

"Good-bye, McCain."

She took her rake and went back to work. Then turned around. "Don't forget what I said about Bill and Rivers. There really may be something there. And you might check out Jeff Cronin too. When Richard disappeared a couple of weeks ago? The night he came stumbling home through the pasture, somebody told us they saw Cronin's Studebaker up on the west hill."

"Richard disappeared?"

"He didn't tell you about that?" She seemed almost curious now. "He missed an important meeting. Maybe, like he told me, it was nothing. Said it was car problems. He got a lift most of the way home. Had to walk the rest of the way. But later I heard Cronin's car had been seen up there the same night. He's the last person Richard would take a ride from."

I wondered if that was what Conners had wanted to tell me. The incident that "required more of an explanation." I'll say it did! Why would Cronin's car be up there? For one thing, it was posted land and Cronin and Richard were enemies. And for another, it was a strange coincidence that Cronin should be up there the night Richard "disappeared."

Chris Tomlin saw me coming. Her little girl was off the tricycle now and running around in noisy circles with the dog.

There aren't fashion magazines for women like her. They defy fashion. Crisp blue button-down shirt. A pair of Sears jeans. Argyle socks. White Keds. Maybe it's the short red hair. Or the tortoise-shell rims on the glasses. But most probably it's the hard wry intelligence in the brown eyes and the hint of wildness in the slightly large mouth. Of course, that fine little body didn't hurt, either. As the paperback writers would say, she gave the impression of being the intellectual sort who had a PhD in S-E-X.

"My ears are burning."

"Gosh," I said.

"You were talking about me, weren't you?"

"You two aren't the best of friends?"

She shook her head. "It's so strange. I'm the one who should be intimidated. I mean, look at her, for God's sake. A goddess. But I guess because our husbands are professional men, she's intimidated by the fact that I have a graduate degree and she doesn't."

"There's more than one way to be intimidated."

She laughed. "I'd swap her that face and body for every single thing I know about T. S. Eliot. Are you working for the Judge?"

"Uh-huh."

"Gosh, am I a suspect?"

"Probably."

"Finally," she said. "Something exciting in my life. Nothing against your little town, but not much happens here."

"A lot of people like it that way."

She shrugged. "Don't I know it. Bill never wants to leave. We have a running battle about it. There are four large universities that would love to have him. And for very, very decent money."

"Maybe he'll change his mind now that Richard's dead."

The giggle-scream. The big collie had playfully knocked the little girl to the ground and was licking her again. The little girl was all balled up to protect herself, rolling back and forth on the grass.

"Excuse me a second," she said, and ran off to redeem her child. "It's all right, Nicole!" she called, as she ran. "Roscoe, you leave her alone now!" Then, when she reached him: "Bad dog! Bad dog!"

She got Nicole to her feet and brushed off her jeans and green sweatshirt. Then she gave Roscoe a talking-to and damned if the dog didn't sit there and look as if he understood every word she was saying.

She set them to playing again. I figured Roscoe was probably good for another two–three minutes before he jumped Nicole and started lapping away on her sweet little face.

"So we were saying—?" she said when she got back.

"I was saying maybe Bill will want to leave, now that Richard's dead."

She looked very serious. "That's going to be interesting. They've been together since college."

"Dana says they've been arguing."

She smirked. "Good old Dana. Did she tell you Bill shot him? That's what she told Cliffie. He came charging over, all ready to arrest poor Bill."

"Bill had an alibi?"

"Yes. But he didn't need one. Think about it. Richard's book was going to be a best-seller. They would've worked out the argument they were having. Bill would have made a small fortune. And it would have given him a great publishing credit.

But not without Richard. Richard had to be alive to promote his biography. The book'll still come out, but it won't have the same impact."

From what I knew of publishing, she was right. The book would be controversial and Richard would have been in great demand for TV and radio interviews.

"So Bill was where when Richard was killed?"

"Walking."

"I see."

"With Nicole and me and Roscoe."

"Ah."

"Down by the river. This time of year, it's so beautiful. You don't look as if you believe me."

"I'll have to check with Nicole."

Her mouth opened in a slow, tempting smile. "Maybe Roscoe would be better. He's very good with alibis."

Just then, Roscoe started barking at the sight of a small green Saab four-door that had pulled into the drive. I could see Bill Tomlin inside. Classical music filled the car. Engine and music died. He got out, carrying his briefcase. He'd gone casual today. Western, actually. Levi's jacket and jeans, work shirt, black Western boots.

"Humor him," she said, as he drew close. "He thinks he's Roy Rogers."

"I keep telling him that I'm the Pecos Kid. He was in an old pulp magazine I read as a kid."

"Pecos never carries a gun—"she smiled, "—just a brief-case."

He kissed her on the cheek. If either of them felt badly about the death of Richard Conners, they were doing a good job of keeping it to themselves. I'd expected them to be an unhappy couple, but the contrary seemed true. The way they kidded each other was spontaneous and intimate.

"McCain here thinks you killed Richard," she said.

He looked right at me and said, "I did."

I must've looked shocked.

"God, I'm kidding. I mean, in my mind I killed Richard hundreds and hundreds of times. And I'm sure he killed me hundreds and hundreds of times, too. I resented his popularity and power, and he resented my mind and my bitching. I'm a past master at bitching, just as he was a past master at being disorganized and forgetting to keep promises he'd made— sometimes very serious promises. We loved each other and hated each other the moment we first met. He never gave me credit enough for what I did for him—and I never gave him credit enough for what he did for me. We both had giant economy-sized egos, I'm afraid. And who knows, maybe some-day one of us would actually have killed the other. We were in very bad need of a divorce, I'm not denying that." Nicole had come toddling over. He bent down and picked her up and kissed her on the cheek. "But I didn't kill him." He grinned at Chris. "I'd be much more likely to kill my wife because she won't leave me alone about moving. I love your little town, McCain, and I want to stay here."

"You knew this Rivers fellow?"

"Knew *of* him. And certainly knew his group, those America First bastards. They've been after Richard for years. But I never met him personally."

"Dana is under the impression that you and Rivers might have been plotting against Richard."

He shook his head. "Poor Dana. So jealous and insecure. All these imaginary plots going on in her mind. The day we went to see Khrushchev, she accused Richard and Chris of having an affair."

It was surprising how different he was away from Richard. The day I'd seen him with Richard at the Khrushchev outing, he'd had the air of a secretary, always walking two steps back, subservient. This was a very different Bill Tomlin. And he'd just explained why Chris and Dana had been arguing that day.

The phone rang inside the house.

"I'd better get that," Chris said.

"I'd better go too, it may be for me."

I looked at them. "You two are handling your grief very well."

"Yes," he said tartly, "aren't we, though?"

I rowed back across the great river just as the first stars appeared in the vermilion-streaked sky of early dusk. The water was cold. But not nearly as cold as the eyes of Chris and Bill Tomlin.

IF YOU LOOK closely at the gravestones and markers, you'll see a lot of them from the 1890s. That decade, at least for Black River Falls, makes you wonder if some dark cosmic force hadn't conspired to punish the town. Two droughts, a long siege of cholera, and—absolutely true—not one but two plagues of crop-destroying grasshoppers. The town's population shrank by about a third during that decade. Not even the Civil War thirty years earlier had reduced the number of residents so severely.

In the 1950s, something along the same lines happened to our little town. But the dark force produced different symptoms and a different name: polio, or infantile paralysis. This plague had been building steadily all century. In a three-month period in 1916, twenty-seven thousand cases were reported in the United States. New York City alone had nine thousand cases. Because nothing else killed as many children as polio, it became the bogeyman for several generations, certainly for mine. Every day at school, you'd see a dozen kids clacking painfully down the hall, metal supports on their legs, crutches tucked under their arms. But as much as you felt sorry for them, there were kids far worse off: in wheelchairs or dying in iron lungs. Summer was the time of terror. You played around other kids—polio being highly communicable—or went to public swimming pools or movie theaters knowing that this might be your unlucky day. Moms and dads swallowed down panic whenever you said you might be running a fever or had a headache or felt a soreness in your muscles.

And then along came a doctor named Jonas Salk, who'd created a polio vaccine. He got permission to try it out in Iowa, as well as two other states, and it worked. I was too old to participate in the trials when Salk's people came to town but I wasn't too old to get drunk the afternoon it was announced that the Salk vaccine had proved effective. The only other thing I can liken it to was the day the war ended. There were celebrations everywhere. The bogeyman had been slain. When Dr. Salk came through town a couple of weeks later, people lined the streets, applauding, and both women and men cried openly. Because of him, their children would be safe. He was a great man. He was offered a New York City ticker tape parade, and he turned it down. I always thought that defined him. His work mattered more than any acclaim.

All this was too late for Robert Emmett McCain, my older brother. He'd died of polio in the fall of 1952. My people are small and Irish, and most of us bear the ineluctable air of immigrants, the sense that we aren't quite good enough to belong here—here being wherever we are. Not Robert Emmett McCain. He was all things to all people: the complete athlete (baseball, basketball, track, and swimming) for the boys; handsome, talented (he had a great singing voice), and playful for the girls; honest and reliable for our folks (he'd taken damned good care of me and my kid sister, Ruthie, when Dad was in the war and Mom was working at the Red Cross). He was going to be the first fully integrated McCain. Not only would he leave the Knolls, the poor section where we lived; he would leave Black River Falls and take his rightful place in the world at large—not unlike Richard Conners.

I still remember the night he got sick at the dinner table. Rushing him to the bathroom. Mom said, with great hope, "He's just been out in the sun too long, that boy." But unspoken was the dread that it was much worse than simple exposure to the sun. Little Ruthie said, "I'll say a prayer for him, Mom." We all said many, many prayers in the days to come. I remember kneeling by my bed so long my knees hurt, hoping God would take those hurting knees into account and spare my brother. But he didn't. It was polio of the most virulent kind. Graham Greene called it "The terrible wisdom of God." Its wisdom was lost on me (I guess that's why only Job, of all the Bible writers, makes a hell of a lot of sense to me), but the suffering Robert went through, only to die suffocating inside his iron lung, was terrible. As was the attendant horror for my folks that maybe Ruthie or I would come down with it next. But we didn't. The Lord spared us.

MOM AND DAD were at Robert's grave when I reached the hill, Crow Creek Hill, high enough to see a long way downriver. Lore has it that squaws stood here for a glimpse of their warriors, coming home from battle in their painted canoes.

Mom and Dad knelt at the grave, the grass browned and sparse with fall. Mom's fingers were rosary-wrapped and she was crying, though softly. Dad's face, which the war had seemed to change so much, was hard. And that's how it had been with them—after my brother's death, I mean—Mom grieving and Dad hard, almost angry. They'd put a bouquet of autumn flowers in front of the stone, Dad shooing away a curious jay intent on closer inspection. The breeze from off the blue winding water below carried a clean scent of fall with it. The birches and cedars along the shore below had started to blaze with the season.

Dad stood up, and I took his place. I gave Mom a kiss on her tear-warm cheek and then addressed myself to my brother. How fine and splendid his life would have been. I'd not only loved him, I'd admired him. And God, how I'd copied him! I wore my hair the way he did, whistled the same songs, crouched in the batter's box the same way, even tried to copy the way he pleased the girls. He always encouraged me. He was a handyman, a good student, and a natural athlete, and he'd been kind enough to pretend that I was all these things too, even though I couldn't pound a nail in straight, never did get the hang of math, and tripped and fell over second base the only time I ever hit a ball into the outfield. He didn't care. I was his kid brother, and he was there to take care of me.

So I said the kind of prayer you say when you're not even sure there's anybody to hear you, fragments of loss and hope and sentiment and emptiness and fear that there's just this beautiful autumn day and nothing else, that the end is really the end, just the cold earth, with no chance of seeing any of the loved ones you've lost along the way. When I thought seriously about life, I always thought about Job, God's imperfect man. I was a lot more like him than I wanted to be. I had not been blessed with blind faith.

After a time, we were all standing up and hugging each other, small Irish people, my mother a beauty still with that wry Myrna Loy wisdom in her blue eyes, my dad starting to wear down after a Depression spent in the Knolls and four years of war overseas.

"Got a letter from Ruthie," Mom said.

"How's she doing?" I asked.

A few months ago, Ruthie had gotten pregnant. Eleventh grade. Unwed mother. Mom had a widowed sister in Chicago. Ruthie went there and her pregnancy was going well. Ruthie had my dead brother's good looks and brains. She'd been planning on Northwestern and then on to New York, and God help all those Manhattan sophisticates when this small town girl started wrapping them around her finger. All that was unlikely now, though it was still a dream we all paid lip-service to. Hard to storm the offices of *Time* or *The New Yorker* with a wee one tucked under your arm.

Then my dad said, "You see that blue Nash down there, honey?"

I smiled. "I thought we had an agreement about that. You agreed to stop calling me honey after I turned twenty-five."

He laughed, and in that moment you could see the kid in his face. I gave him a hug. He always loved to tell the story of how he'd dropped me off at a Rocky Lane–Gene Autry–Whip Wilson triple feature at the theater one Saturday afternoon and forgot himself and gave me a kiss as I was about to get out of the car. Right in front of all the other nine-year-olds in the ticket line. "I still feel like hell about it, though, honey," he'd always say. "I never saw a kid blush the way you did that day."

"She got out a pair of binoculars about ten minutes ago," he said. "Aimed right up here. You don't know who she is?"

"I wish you didn't have to work for the Judge," Mom said. "She doesn't care how dangerous things get for you."

"I'll be fine, Mom. Really." I kissed her, and then I gave Dad a peck on the cheek. " 'Bye, honey," I said to him, and he gave me a mock punch in the belly. "Look, Mom, Dad's blushing."

I stepped over to the grave and touched it a final time. So long, Robert.

Then I walked over to my car. I wanted to find out who the woman in the Nash was.

I CALLED JEFF Cronin's office. Wasn't in. I swung out to his house, a new ranch style that was set about two hundred yards away from the other homes in the development, as if it didn't want to get contaminated. The woman in the Nash stayed a long, respectable block behind me.

Jeff's black Studebaker—the one that looked even more like a spaceship than the Edsel—sat basking in its own glory in the driveway. Cronin, like Dana and Dorothy, was raking leaves and putting them into bags that his wife, Jane, helped him with, a plump but sweet-faced woman. He had a couple of cast-iron deer in the front and an American flag flapping on a pole.

He stopped raking the moment he saw me pull into his drive. We weren't exactly friends. I saw him say something to his wife and wave her inside the house. The antichrist was coming.

I knew enough not to try and shake hands. He'd decline.

He was chunky but strong-looking, wearing the same black burr cut he'd had as a fishing-pole prairie kid. His gray sweatshirt was sweaty in the armpits. His jeans were baggy and faded.

"I'm not changing my mind," he said, "in case that's why you're here."

"Changing your mind about what?"

He looked surprised. "About Helen Toricelli. Howard Fast is on every list of communist sympathizers I've ever seen." He spat. "Communist sympathizers, my ass. They're communists and everybody knows it. But you have to be careful because they can sue you."

"She's a fine woman. She was raised in the Depression. She saw a lot of people starve. She doesn't want to see that again, so she looks around for ways to prevent it. She reads a lot of different things and shares her thoughts with her students. She's one of the best teachers I've ever known. And one of the nicest people, too."

"I'm going to surprise you here, Sam, and agree with you. About being a nice woman. She's salt of the earth. That's why this doesn't make me happy. I've talked to her a dozen times about not teaching some of the material she does, but she refuses to quit. As a school board member, what choice do I have? I've got to try and get rid of her for the sake of our kids."

Then he wagged his head toward the back yard. I followed him. In a side window I saw his wife, Jane, peeking out between the curtains, probably trying to figure out where we were headed.

The back yard was fenced off with white pickets. There was a swing set, an outdoor grill, and a wheelchair. In the wheelchair was a man—or what was left of a man, anyway. Lew Cronin had been a soldier in Korea. A lieutenant. He was captured and held for two years. The Koreans brainwashed him so severely there wasn't much left of him. Killing him would have been kinder. They sent him back after the war. After a proper interval, his wife divorced him and moved away, taking the kids. He probably wasn't even aware of it. He was usually in the psychiatric hospital. Sometimes, he stayed here with his brother. They had a place fixed up for him in the basement. He rarely spoke, just stared. Sat in his wheelchair and stared. I wondered if he knew how beautiful the day was. Or how sweet the breeze. Or how romantic the leaves burning near by.

"There's your communism for you."

I wanted to hate him but I couldn't. Would I have been any different if Lew had been my brother?

"The sonsabitches," he said. "Ten times a day, I want to get my hands on them."

"Helen Toricelli didn't have anything to do with this."

"No. But the people who wrote those books did."

Jane came to the back door. "Time to wash up for supper. . . . Hi, Sam."

"Hi, Jane."

"Dorothy Conners probably won't believe this but she's in my prayers," Jane said. "I didn't care much for her boy, but I always liked Dana."

I wanted to hate her the way I wanted to hate him. Their hatred had made them fanatics. Then they'd shock you with their decent side.

"Thanks, Jane."

He said, "I'm sorry, Sam. I'm still going through with it."

He was looking toward the door. Supper, whatever it was, sure smelled good. "I'm told you were up in the pastureland the night Richard Conners came back home a couple weeks ago."

"Who the hell told you that?"

"Doesn't matter. It true?"

He was back to the unfriendly man I was familiar with. "Don't push me, McCain. I'm the wrong man to push. Believe me."

He didn't once turn around. Went to the back steps. Opened the back door. Went inside.

On the way back to my car, I slowed down so I could get a good look at the tread on the Studebaker tires.

I DECIDED TO make things simple for both of us.

I started to walk to my car, but then I passed it and ended up where she was parked in her nice blue Nash.

I went over to the driver's side. She was reading a copy of *Time* with Khrushchev's photo on it. She was one of those

petite little women; everything about her was petite and delicate, from her earnest, smart, pretty face to her tiny wrists to
the precise little knees that showed below the line of her black
dress. She had a perky black hat on that set her blond hair off
nicely.

"Hi," I said.

She looked up and smiled. She had baby teeth. Sweet and
sexy. "Hi. Am I supposed to know you?"

"Gee, by now I'd think we're sort of old friends."

"We are?"

"Sure. You've been following me around all day. My dad
even saw you watching me through binoculars."

"That is a great pickup line, you know? But then, being that
you're so short and all, you probably *need* great pickup lines,
don't you?"

The patter would've been more believable if her azure blue
eyes hadn't been tinted red from recent tears. I wondered why
she'd been crying.

I opened her door.

"I could always call a cop," she said.

"Believe me, you wouldn't want to call a cop in this town."

"Exactly why did you open my door?" she said, irritation in
her voice now.

"Because we're going to go have a very civilized cup of coffee, and then you're going to tell me who the hell you are and
why you're following me."

NINE

I'M SORRY I SAID you were short," she said, twenty
minutes later, over coffee.

"I *am* short," I said.

"I know. But it hurt your feelings."

"No, it didn't."

"Sure it did. I could see it in your eyes. You have very expressive eyes."

I smiled.

"What's funny about having very expressive eyes?" she said.

"When I was in high school, I tried to train myself to get
used to insults. I'd stand in front of the mirror and say, 'Your
problem, McCain, is you're short. You're short, McCain, you
hear that? *Short!*' I figured if I said it enough, the word would
lose its effect on me."

"Did it work?"

"No. It still hurt my feelings and embarrassed me every time
somebody said it." I smiled again. "I think my expressive eyes
gave me away."

"They're nice eyes."

"So're yours."

"Thanks. They're probably my best feature."

"You're very pretty, too."

"Pretty, maybe. *Very* pretty, no. And lots of girls are pretty. So that isn't anything special."

We were in Al Monahan's Downtown Café. Al lost both his legs in Guam but that didn't stop him from running the best restaurant in town. Best meat loaf in the county, though men are careful never to say that to their wives or mothers. While Al has a staff, he does a lot of the work himself. He zips around in his wheelchair, usually with a pot of hot coffee for refills in his right hand.

"So," I said. "This is the part where you tell me who you are and why you're following me."

"I'd rather talk about you than me."

"I'm not very interesting."

"You work for an aristocratic judge. You have a private investigator's license but would rather practice law. The love of your life just ran off with the love of *her* life. There's a sweet girl who works down the street at Rexall named Mary who's in love with you. Your sister got pregnant and had to move to Chicago. You like to read paperback crime novels, Peter Rabe and John D. MacDonald especially, though lately you've been on a Harry Whittington kick."

"Harry Whittington? How in God's name did you find that out?"

"On the stand next to your bed. Five Harry Whittington Gold Medal books. I'd call that a kick, wouldn't you?"

"Then you broke into my apartment?"

She had a radiant smile. "Broke implies a certain lack of finesse. Let's just say I let myself in. Twice, in fact. One of the Whittingtons looked very interesting. *Brute in Brass.*"

"It's probably his best book. Why didn't you just steal it?"

"I'm not a thief, Sam."

"Oh? Then what are you?"

She sipped coffee. I caught Al's eye and raised my cup. He whizzed over. Freshened up both our cups. "How'd you like the roast beef sandwich yesterday?" Al said to her.

"Best I ever had."

"This is a good one, Sam," he said, winking at me. "Pretty *and* smart."

"That's one thing I'll always like about your country," she said, when he'd gone. "The majority of people have the opportunity to better themselves no matter what has happened to them. He has a great little restaurant here."

I said, "*My* country. You're not from here?"

"Not originally, no."

"From where?"

"Good. You can't tell. That means my accent is entirely gone. Finally." Then, before I could ask another question, she said, "The only thing I don't like is all the violence. Even in a small town like this one. Two murders within twenty-four hours. Richard Conners and a man named—"

"Not a man," I said, my damaged pride suddenly raw again, "a jerk—a jerk named Rivers."

Now it was my turn to notice *her* expressive eyes and the way she winced when I called Rivers a jerk. Very simply, she said, "Rivers was my brother."

I knew now why she'd just finished crying when I'd first walked back to her car.

IN 1934, THE ever-paranoid Joseph Stalin was looking for a way to launch a purge. An idealistic young man in Leningrad named Sergei Kirov was developing a following that Stalin did not like. Unlike Stalin, whose only concern was staying in power, and who had murdered millions of Russians in order to do so, Kirov was a true man of the people. Stalin saw Kirov and people like him as a threat. So he devised an idea that would take care of Kirov *and* his growing number of followers. He employed an assassin named Leonid Nikolaev to murder Kirov. In turn, Nikolaev was killed by Stalin, who then announced that the country needed to be purged of all of Nikolaev's subversive cohorts. He did this in the guise of praising Kirov, even going so far as to erect a statue to him in Moscow. He used this pretext to launch what became known in Russian history as the Time of Great Terror, to purge the country of *all* those who disagreed with him. Hundreds of thousands of people were killed. Near Karelia alone—a picturesque republic in northwest Russia—more than nine thousand bodies of political prisoners were later discovered.

To be associated in any way with the assassin Nikolaev meant eventual death. To be related to him meant *swift* death. Karl Rivers and his sister Natalie had come to the United States as small children in 1937, she said. Their father and mother had smuggled them to freedom. But even before they could leave the Soviet Union, they saw their mother shot by a secret police officer and their father shipped off to a notorious gulag on the Moscow-Volga canal that would be a monument to both engineering and tyranny. They never heard from their father again.

Brother and sister grew up in New York City. In-laws raised them to be—understandably—anti-Stalinist, anticommunist. Natalie absorbed these sentiments without becoming fanatical about them. Her brother became psychotic (her word) about the Bolshevik empire. He enlisted to serve in the Korean War, risking his life many times, earning many ribbons and citations for bravery, including the Distinguished Service Cross. He went into the FBI, where he became, according to J. Edgar himself, the "ideal" agent. Then, two years ago, he became involved with a group called America First. Many wealthy and influential men were said to have established this organization, though none would publicly lend his name to it. The group's goal was simple: to "purge" (a familiar word) local communities of communists and communist sympathizers (comsymps).

They concentrated on city halls, school boards and libraries. They boasted that more than a thousand public servants had been turned out of their positions in the first eight months alone. They worked both openly (in citizen groups who showed up at council and school board meetings to denounce suspect officials) and covertly (with pamphlets that frequently cited Jewish, Catholic, and civil rights organizations as communist fronts). A little over a year ago, Richard Conners had denounced the group by name on a CBS radio interview. The group had made him its number-one target.

"WHAT WAS YOUR brother doing out here?"

"I don't know. We hadn't spoken in months."

"Why not?"

"He has—had—a wife and two sweet little girls. He got so involved in America First that he virtually deserted them. I took their side in the matter. He resented it, said I was disloyal, said that as a Russian immigrant I should understand how important his work was."

"You didn't approve of what he was doing?"

"I always put it this way. I'm sure there are Russian spies in the highest positions in Washington. And Russian spies all around the country. And they must be identified and dealt with. But all this hysteria—Joe McCarthy and groups like America First—they're doing exactly what the Russians want: turning people against each other, creating distrust everywhere. I'm all for an orderly, honest investigation to expose the Russian spies in this country. But—"

"I can see where you might've had some disagreements with your brother."

"I truly believe that by the end he was mentally ill."

"I'm sorry I called him a jerk."

"I'm afraid that's exactly what he became."

"And now you're out here to—"

"Find out why he was killed. And who killed him."

"The police chief seems to think maybe I did it."

"Your police chief is an idiot."

"You noticed?"

"My brother went to your apartment looking for something. Somebody followed him there and killed him."

"That's the way I see it, too."

"I want to help you, Sam. I owe it to my brother. I loved him. Well, I hated him *and* I loved him. That's the worst feeling in the world."

"Yeah, I think it is."

"I can help you. I know how America First operates. And I have some idea of what he might have been doing out here."

"Yeah? What?"

"This is just speculation. You asked me before why he was here and I said I didn't know. And I don't. Not for sure. But I do know what he did in the past. And that was to get people to confess that they were secretly communists."

"How did he do that?"

"The America First people used him for two reasons. First, because he was great window dressing, a former FBI agent who'd also lived under communist oppression."

"And second?"

"Because he was an expert at torture. He'd studied the methods of the KGB. He became just like the people he hated."

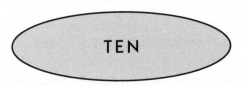

TEN

We stopped by my apartment on the way to the motel where Rivers had been staying. Mrs. Goldman had been nice enough to spend the day cleaning. She left a note saying she'd appreciate it if I'd help her rake leaves next week. Two windows were half open and there was a nice breeze.

Natalie sat on the couch. The cats liked her, Tash on her lap, Crystal and Tess on either side, all well within stroking distance.

"This is a nice place," Natalie said. "Cozy."

"You wouldn't have said that this morning."

"I wonder if they found anything."

"I didn't have anything to find."

"They obviously think you did. Maybe something that Conners gave you."

"He didn't give me anything."

"Maybe he dropped it off and you didn't know about it. Or maybe he put it in the mail and it hasn't arrived yet."

In the john, I changed out of my suit into desert boots, chinos, a crew-neck blue sweater, and a brown leather aviation-style jacket.

"You look cute," she said.

"So do you."

"You don't always have to compliment me when I compliment you."

"Compliment me some more and I'll see if I can remember that."

She helped me fill up the cat bowls. The kitty sand she allowed me to do solo.

ECONO-MILES WAS LOCATED on the way to Iowa City. It was one of those postwar prefabs that started to disintegrate the day it opened for business. Roof, walls, walks all showed signs of hurried patchwork repairs. Several of the cars parked in front of the rooms had fins like sharks. They'd be needing hurried patchwork repairs soon, too. I'd take my Ford any day over those Detroit nightmares.

The woman behind the registration desk was watching a TV news break. A senator was saying that he had strong suspicions that Fidel Castro wasn't a friend of democracy after all but a full-blown communist. The woman took a long drag on her Kool filter tip and frowned. Her name was Esther Haley. She was one of those worn but somehow ageless women—born age fifty-two—and hadn't changed her hairstyle, her makeup (Jean Harlow plucked eyebrows), or put-upon frown since then. She looked at Natalie and then at me and said, "C'mon, McCain, you know this ain't no hot-sheet place."

Natalie laughed. "That's great. I'm always worried I look like such a prig. Now I know I look like a B-girl."

"We're here to ask you some questions, Esther. About Rivers, the guy who was murdered last night."

"Not a nice guy."

"This is his sister, Esther," I said. "Go a little easy."

"It's all right," Natalie said. "We want the truth."

"Well, that's the truth, honey. Very abrasive. Very pushy. That was Karl. I'm sorry for what happened to him."

"He have any visitors?" I said.

"Only one time that I know of. They had some kind of row."

"How do you know that?"

"Salesman in the next room called down and said he was gonna ask for his money back if they didn't quit yellin' in there. I was fillin' in for Fred, the nightman. He's got some kind of throat ailment. So he says anyway. Lazy bastard, if you ask me. Anyway, I called your brother's room and told him to knock it off or I'd call the cops and have them throw him out."

"He quiet down?"

"Yeah."

"Any idea who all was in his room?"

"Nope. But I walked down there and took a gander down the row. There was three cars and a couple trucks and motor-cycles."

"You hear them arguing?"

"Not when I walked down there."

"So no other visitors or problems?"

She shook her graying head. "I'm sorry if I insulted your brother, miss," she said.

Natalie offered a sad smile. "Oh, that's all right. I used to insult him myself."

SOMEBODY ONCE SAID all crowds are potential lynch mobs. Takes very little to turn them in that direction. I must instinctively believe that because crowds make me nervous. I sense their capacity for violence.

There was a crowd gathered around the front doors of the high school in the early autumn evening, the stars cold and hard and beautiful in the gray-washed sky. Headlights washed across the faces of the people—good people, our people, *my* people—angry now, on one side or the other, about teacher Helen Toricelli. Seeing her as a communist—or even left-wing—was laughable. But Black River Falls hadn't been spared the hysteria of the decade. Even with McCarthy gone, his work was being carried on.

As Natalie and I approached the two-story red brick building where I had spent four years reading paperback crime novels hidden in my schoolbooks, I saw that the crowd was divided not only emotionally but physically, too. They argued back and forth across a gap of three or four feet, the cleared area leading to the steps and indoors. This was going to be a nasty night. Nothing's meaner than a family brawl, and that's what this was going to be. Because the town was a family. People here had known each other since birth. Grown up together. Married each other. Went into business together. Buried each other. And now fools like Jeff Cronin were turning them against each other.

The school had that autumn smell, wooden floors recently shellacked, walls freshly painted, a new school year. The meeting was in the gym. A long table in front of the stage, folding chairs fanned out to face it. The chairs were filled already. Again, the pro–Helen Toricelli people on one side, the against–Helen Toricelli people on the other. The gym was multipurpose. It was used for penny carnivals, proms, sock hops, assemblies, charity dances, voting booths, political gatherings, and even, upon occasion, a basketball game.

Helen herself was here already. She sat in the front row, right on the aisle. There was an empty chair between her and the next person. She looked isolated, the way, as a sad-eyed, gangly spinster, she'd been isolated all her life. Natalie and I found chairs at the back. Then I excused myself and went up to see Helen.

"Thanks for coming, McCain," she said, when she saw me. "I need all the help I can get. I think Cronin'll probably suggest I get shipped straight over to Moscow tonight."

"Cronin's an ass."

She smiled. She sure was homely, buck-toothed, wall-eyed, big-nosed homely, yet there was a sweet sorrow in that face that gave it true dignity. I couldn't help myself. I reached out and gave her a hug.

"You better be careful. People'll start talking about us."

"Let them talk."

"If only you'd been a better student. I hated giving you all those C's. But you did better in college. Otherwise you wouldn't have gotten through law school."

"I didn't read as many Mickey Spillane novels in college as I did in high school."

She smiled. "You and those darn twenty-five-cent paperbacks of yours."

The school board filed in through a side door. Like most politicians, they usually spent time working the room: waving, pointing, grinning. Jus' folks, that's us. But not tonight. Tight, unhappy faces. All business. There'd be no waving and grinning tonight. The Helen Toricelli matter had changed all that.

Charles DeWitt, board chairman, raised his hand to silence the chatter. The sides weren't arguing back and forth across the aisle but they were talking loudly among themselves. Each side had a mix of farmers, laborers, business people. The age spread was similarly varied, from twenty to ninety.

DeWitt said, "I want to tell you people something. I seriously considered resigning tonight. The members of the board asked me to stay on and I did. But I want to warn you: If this meeting

tonight gets as ugly as some of the mail I've been getting, I plan
to quit on the spot and walk right out that door. I like to think
this is a special little town and that whatever disagreements we
have can be settled peacefully. But it's like this 'red scare' stuff
makes otherwise sensible people crazy." He nodded in the direction of the door he'd just come in. "So I just want to make
myself clear. I'm prepared to walk right out that door anytime
I think this meeting's getting out of hand."

Somebody said, "Where's Cronin?"

A tiny woman who looked like an angry bird stood up and
said, "Jeff Cronin is supposed to present our side in the matter,
Mr. DeWitt. He told me just this afternoon that he has evidence that Miss Toricelli has been a member of several groups
the Attorney General of the United States has labeled subversive"—she consulted a list in her hand—"including the National Committee for Freedom of the Press, the National Labor
Council for Peace, and the People's Drama League." She
looked right at Helen Toricelli. "Miss Toricelli was one of my
teachers, and I want to go on record as saying that I have a
lot of affection for her and respect for her abilities in the class-
room. But given her communistic leanings, I don't think she
should be allowed to teach our children any longer."

The subversive list she read from was notorious. It targeted
Negro, Jewish, immigrant, and left-wing Catholic organizations almost exclusively, especially those having to do with the
arts.

"What we're going to do tonight," DeWitt said, "is hear
both sides and then vote in private on whether Helen Toricelli
should be retained by this school district."

"He means a 'secret' vote, just like the Kremlin," Fritz
Krause said. He was Cronin's stalking horse on the school
board. "I think we should have the vote tonight, and it should
be right out in the open."

His supporters broke into applause.

"Where is Mr. Cronin?" DeWitt said.

Nobody had a good answer. He was late. Obviously, he was the man of the moment. It was up to him to make his charges against Helen, and then her attorney, a grand old man named Ralph Patterson, would rebut.

Ten, fifteen, twenty minutes went by.

Both sides were anxious and starting to get restless. People started drifting outside to have smokes.

"I can't believe he'd miss an opportunity like this," Natalie said. "He's got the audience he wants just waiting for him."

"Damned strange," I said. "This is his big night. There are six reporters in the back of the room and trucks from two TV stations. I wonder where the hell he is."

About every ten minutes, DeWitt would say, "Has anybody heard from Mr. Cronin?" But his people would just look confused and uneasy.

"Maybe something happened to him," Fritz Krause said in his best ominous tones. "Maybe somebody didn't want him to show up at this meeting."

"Maybe Khrushchev was hiding in the bushes," somebody else said, "and jumped him."

Our side of the aisle laughed a lot at that one. The other side glowered.

I kept glancing at Helen Toricelli. Straight and proud, she sat—out of fashion clothes-wise, out of favor with some of the townspeople she'd served so well over the years. Patterson sat next to her now, and they talked every once in a while.

A woman came in from the back of the room. She wore an ID badge that said FACULTY. She walked up to the committee and said something to them. Then she turned back to us and left the room.

Talk started up again. What had she said? Were they withholding information from us? Fritz Krause, all six-two and two hundred and fifty crew-cut pounds of him, got up from behind the table and took the same path out of the gym that the FACULTY woman had. He didn't say anything. He kept his eyes straight ahead. He didn't even glance over at his own supporters when they called his name.

A woman on our side raised her hand.

"Yes?" DeWitt said.

"What the heck is going on here? Most of us have kids and housework. We can't sit here all night for no good reason."

"Mr. Krause has been called to the phone."

"Do you know why?"

"Not exactly, Louise. I believe Mrs. Cronin called him."

"Mrs. Cronin? But you don't know why?"

"I'm hoping Mr. Krause will explain that when he comes back."

Confusion. Speculation. Irritation. I kept checking my watch. I was supposed to meet Dana at the gate where Cronin's car had been the other night. I was still curious about what he'd been doing in a pasture. He was a city boy. And especially on the night Richard Conners had shown up following a mysterious absence.

A man on the other side addressed DeWitt. "I was told that the school board is picking up the charges for Miss Toricelli's attorney."

"Then you were told wrong," DeWitt said. "And we're not paying for Mr. Cronin's lawyer, either."

The man had wanted an argument—maybe just to kill time while we all waited for Fritz Krause to come back—and he looked disappointed.

When Fritz came back, he didn't look good. He looked, in fact, angry and troubled. What could Mrs. Cronin have said to upset him?

He took his seat again and started whispering in DeWitt's ear.

"I thought you were the one who didn't want any secrets," one of his own supporters shouted at him.

A lot of people shouted their agreement.

DeWitt held his hand up for silence. "Fritz is going to explain what's going on here. So let's have quiet, please."

Fritz Krause said, "I don't want nobody to ask me any questions after I say my piece. Because I don't have any more idea of what's going on than you do. All I know for sure is that a few minutes ago on the phone in the faculty lounge, Jeff's wife told me he's disappeared. She doesn't know where he is. She sounded worried." Krause paused, and when he continued, he sounded more uncomfortable than worried. "Jeff had information pertinent to the investigation of Helen Toricelli. We can't conduct this hearing without him."

What the hell was this all about?

I obviously wasn't the only one asking the question. The crowd fell again into verbal chaos.

"We stuck our necks out and supported him," a man sitting on the other side said. "What the hell's going on here?"

"I told you. No questions. I don't know any more than you do. I just know what Mrs. Cronin told me. And what she told me, I just told you."

DeWitt stood up. "I move that we adjourn this meeting. Is there a second?"

One of the board members raised her hand.

"I appreciate your interest in this matter," DeWitt said, "but maybe it's just as well that it ends like this."

"Oh, it ain't over," said a particularly angry man. "Not by a long shot, it ain't."

His mood proved typical of the anti–Helen Toricelli crowd that gathered outside. There were even a few brief scuffles among men on opposing sides of the issue.

"These people scare me," Natalie whispered, putting her arm through mine.

"Yeah," I said, feeling that I was betraying my own towns-people, "they scare me, too."

WITH THE TOP down on my ragtop, and the going slow because the gravel road out here in the country was rutted from recent rains, you could hear the farm animals settling in for the night: horses, cows, pigs. My uncle had this horse once who snored so loud you could hear him from the house if you kept the windows open on a summer night.

"May I ask you something?" Natalie said.

"Sure."

"This woman who left you, this Pamela, aren't you in great pain?"

"Yeah. About every fifteen minutes it hits me."

"A Dartmouth boy left me for a Smith girl one winter, and I couldn't get out of bed for a month. It was very dramatic. I felt purely Russian for the first time since I'd come to the States." She paused. "You hide it very well, your pain."

"I've had practice."

"Oh?"

"She's broken my heart somewhere in the vicinity of three thousand times. You never get used to it, but you get better at handling it."

Then we were there. With all the new silos and barns and metal outbuildings, most of the countryside looked different these days. When I was growing up, you could go places that hadn't changed much since the Indians had wandered here un-troubled a couple of centuries earlier, before French trappers reached the Mississippi River, sixty miles to the east.

This back pasture had none of the modern accoutrements except for barbed wire fencing. Heavy dark rain clouds kept obscuring the moon. With a forest nearby and pastureland before us rolling up toward the dark empty hills, it had a feeling of isolation. What would Jeff Cronin be doing out here? If he was going to eavesdrop on the Connerses, he certainly would have gotten closer to their house. This field was a good mile from the farm itself. It didn't make any sense.

We heard her before we saw her.

There was something timeless and thrilling about the sound of the solitary rider and horse in the shadows before us. It was a noise—the hooves and the heaving chest of the animal—heard upon this land for centuries.

She dismounted easily, with the experienced rider's disdain for perfect form; she simply dropped to the ground. In her blue suede jacket, white shirt, and jeans and a goddess's head of blond hair, she was the Potomac's version of the grand prize in the young-beautiful-wife sweepstakes. Out here the grand prizes tend to have dimples and cuddly breasts and say inanely cute things. In Washington, D.C., they discuss Sartre and foreign policy and dare you to make a move on their fierce, slim bodies.

"Sorry I'm late," Dana Conners said, more civil than usual. "Chris and I were having a little disagreement."

"You were having a disagreement two days ago when we saw you at the Garst farm with Khrushchev," I said. "You shoved her, in fact."

"She had it coming, believe me." Before I could say anything more, she put out her hand to Natalie and said, "I'm Dana Conners. And you are—?"

I introduced them properly.

"I'm sorry about your brother," Dana said. Then: "Oh,

what a hypocrite I'm being. I'm not sorry about your brother at all. He was our enemy. And I think he had something to do with my husband's murder."

"I'm not going to defend my brother," Natalie said. "I can't. But I can mourn him. I owe him that. I know what you're going through with your husband's death," she added.

Dana nodded.

I turned on my flashlight. "I checked the back weather reports. Three hours before Cronin's car was seen up here, it rained. So it should be easy to find some tire tracks. He drives a new Studebaker. I checked the tread on his tires: a diamond pattern."

Dana said to Natalie, "Impressive, isn't he?"

Natalie laughed. "So far, anyway."

I walked back to the gate and started playing my light around on the ground. The grass thinned as I began walking back toward the two women. Then, in areas of open soil, the tire tracks appeared. They didn't reach out and sock you in the knee for attention, but they were there when you got down on your haunches and looked for them. Diamond-shaped tread.

Then, as I reached the section where grass was growing heavily, the tracks disappeared. I was halfway to the women. It was one of those nights that were alternately muggy and chilly. It smelled of fresh, good earth.

"Any luck?" Dana said.

"Yeah."

"Well, then, at least we can ask Cronin to explain what he was doing out here."

I didn't say anything. I'd found another long patch of soil. At the halfway point in this stretch, the tire tracks stopped. For some reason, Cronin had parked here. Above me now, hidden in the overcast sky, a big commercial airliner roared through the night.

I looked around, trying to see a reason for Cronin to park here.

Then I saw the footprints. In the criminology course I took while getting my private investigator's license, one of the guest speakers—they brought in detectives from all over this part of the state—talked about how the footprint was too often over-looked as evidence. The professor said that Indians had been reading footprints for centuries, hence their abilities as trackers. Footprints not only told you the direction somebody was headed in, they also told you about weight and height and even certain characteristics about the person's walking patterns. In modern times, they also told you the size and type of shoe. Tread on the sole was a good means of identification. Take two pairs of seemingly identical shoes. They won't be identical for long. Each person wears shoes differently—length of stride, angle of wear on the heel—and thus creates a mark as singular as a fingerprint.

I could follow the footsteps from the car. A single set of prints. One man walking to the back of the car. Then there were two sets of prints. Both were pointed toward the front of the car along the passenger side.

"Here's something interesting," I said.

They'd been talking. Now they came over.

"You find something?" Dana said.

I showed her the outline I'd constructed. "Here'd be the front of the car. He walks to the back—follow the flashlight here—and all the time there's a single set of footprints. But now look."

I played my light on what I wanted them to see. "Suddenly, there's a second set of footprints."

"Did somebody else drive in?" Natalie asked.

I trained my light on the long patch of earth behind the end of the car. "No new tire tracks. Just Cronin's."

"But where—?" Dana started to say. Then: "The trunk."

"Exactly."

"He had somebody in the trunk?" Natalie said. "Richard Conners!"

"You said he'd been missing and wasn't sure where he'd been."

Dana said, "But why would Cronin kidnap him?"

"That's what we need to ask him. I think he turned him loose right here. Then Richard walked the rest of the way to your farmhouse."

"But why wouldn't he remember any of this?"

"Shock, trauma, who knows? It happens."

Dana shook her head. "I wonder if anybody told Cronin that kidnapping is a capital offense."

I said, "I'd like to finish talking about Chris."

"Chris is none of your business, McCain."

"Why did you shove her the other day?"

"That's none of your business either."

"It may have something to do with your husband's murder."

"It doesn't." Then, changing the subject again, "How did that stupid school board meeting go tonight, by the way?"

"Cronin didn't show up."

"What?" She looked and sounded genuinely surprised. "After all the hell he's been raising, he didn't show up?" And then an odd look came across her face, as if a remarkable idea had just occurred to her. "I mean, that's strange, isn't it?" But the fire of her initial response was gone. And now there was a sense of agitation about her.

Natalie said, "The police gave me some of my brother's belongings. Would you like to look through them, Sam?"

"Thanks."

We'd left the question of Chris hanging again. Why had

Dana shoved her the other day? And why did Dana ease past the subject of Cronin now?

I went back over the tire prints. Cronin had come in here, yanked Conners from the trunk, and sent him staggering on his way home. Conners wouldn't remember any of it. Conners had probably been drugged, and that inevitably involved Natalie's brother, but what had they been after? Did they get it? And if they got it, what and where was it?

In the distance, you could see the lights of town. Nothing made me feel better than coming home late at night from a trip to Cedar Rapids or Iowa City and seeing those lights. It was like one of those science fiction stories where you can travel back in time to a town that hasn't changed from the good old days. Maybe Black River Falls wasn't ideal, but it was still a town of good people with good hearts for the most part, which had made this whole "red scare" thing so difficult for everybody. All you could liken it to was the Civil War where, in places like Missouri and lower Kansas, families split down the middle, one half blue, the other half gray. Nearly a hundred years later, the spiritual wounds of that war were still with us. The wounds of the McCarthy era threatened to last just as long. Some people I liked and admired had said a lot of ignorant and nasty things about some other people I liked and admired.

Dana still looked preoccupied and eager to leave. "Just close the gate behind you, McCain. I need to get back." She swept up on her horse. "It was nice to meet you, Natalie. Despite the circumstances."

And then she was gone, not trying for drama, but how could you miss, all that icy beauty astride a horse in the dead of night?

We watched her ride away until she was lost in the prairie shadows.

"You like her, Sam?"

"Not much."

"Me either. I wanted to feel sorry for her. Because of her husband. But I couldn't quite—I resent strong women. Probably because I've never been very strong."

I laughed. "Kiddo, you're strong enough to chew on barbed wire." I slid my arm around her shoulder and gave her a brotherly kiss on the cheek. "Look at everything you've survived in your life. Not many people have to face up to what you have."

She slid her arm around my waist. "That doesn't make me strong, Sam. It just means that God has blessed me. Or aren't you religious?"

"Most of the time. In my own sort of way."

"Now there's a deep profession of faith."

I looked up at the few stars in the overcast night. The vast loneliness that is the religious impulse—as opposed to the church impulse, which is about social rules—overcame me, and I had a racial memory (probably owing to all the wonderful Edgar Rice Burroughs books I'd read as a kid) of man in his various incarnations—lizardlike, monkeylike, Cro-Magnon—standing here just as I stood here, looking at the same stars, and feeling the same vast loneliness. Millions and millions of years later, and still, for all our inventions, we faced at least once a day that quick inconsolable grief of wondering why we'd been born and what, if anything, it meant. "I *want* to believe. I really do."

"If I didn't have my faith, I wouldn't have anything."

And then we were making out.

Now, you probably wouldn't think a discussion of faith could lead to making out, but it did. And notice I didn't say "And then we were kissing," because it went way past kissing right into open-mouthed, groin-pressing, hair-raking making out.

It happened just that fast. And God, was she a good kisser! During my short time with her, I'd had the stray sexual thought but then the rational side countered that it was nothing serious because I was too pained about good ol' beautiful Pamela to do anything *about* stray sexual thoughts.

Boy, was I wrong.

Where we ended up was in the back seat of the ragtop. With the top up. She asked if I had a "thing." I said yes—the emergency thing in my billfold, right next to my photo of John Foster Dulles—and then we were making sweet sad love because that happened to be the mood upon us. Healing love. She was a quiet lover, fragile in some ways, and when we were done she said, "Sometimes I can get pretty wild."

"So can I," I said. "I play the banjo."

She laughed. "While you're making love?"

"Just at the pinnacle moment."

"No wonder women are so crazy about you."

"Yes, they are, aren't they?"

When we were dressed again, we stayed in the back seat and she sat on my lap. It felt completely natural and comfortable. Sat on my lap with her arms around my neck, smoking a cigarette and giving me a drag every so often.

She said, "Are you thinking of Pamela?"

"No."

"Liar."

"Well, not very often."

"I ruin all my relationships with jealousy. I'm too possessive."

"That's where the banjo comes in handy."

"The banjo helps with jealousy?"

"Every time you have a jealous thought, you just play."

She laughed. "Will you let me stay with you tonight?"

"I'll have to think it over. Yes," I said. "I've thought it over."

ELEVEN

B OY, IF YOU THOUGHT that one was crazy, listen to this one."

It was 2 A.M. We should've been asleep. We'd stopped at an all-night grocery and bought some hamburger and buns and onions, ketchup and mustard and pickles. She said that making love always made her feel domestic. She also bought a couple of magazines, and that's what we were doing now that we'd eaten and made love a second time—a much more ferocious outing this time—sitting naked in the middle of my bed with two Luckies burning in an ashtray and "Johnny's Greatest Hits" playing low in the background.

She was reading from an "Advice For Teenagers" column, and the exchange was hilarious.

"The name of this one is 'What to Tell Your Teen-Age Daughter About Sex.' You ready, McCain?"

"Ready."

" 'Question: Boys say they don't want their wives to be virgins any more. Is virginity out of date? Answer: The sex act is often painful at first and not pleasurable at all. Therefore if you have sexual intercourse at an early age you may be frightened and disgusted by it—and never marry.' "

"Oh, my God," I said, "you'll probably end up a lesbo." Lesbo was a word you encountered in a lot of Midwood and Beacon paperbacks, the really steamy ones. *Lesbo Lust, Lesbo Love, Lesbo Loonies.* You know the kind of book. The ones you won't admit you read.

"Here's another good one, McCain. This has very specific advice. 'Question: Is there a perfect good night kiss for teenage girls? Answer: Yes, ten seconds—not too long and not too hard.' "

"I'll refrain from commenting on that not-too-long, not-too-hard thing."

"Oh, listen to this!" She was already laughing even before reading it. " 'Question: Is there one type of girl that just about every boy likes? Answer: Yes, indeed. Boys like girls who are peppy and wide awake and who like to have fun.' "

And then the phone rang.

The cats, who'd been sleeping at the foot of the bed, jumped up like a gymnastic team. I had about the same reaction. I'd been so entranced by this sexual advice that the ring scared the hell out of me.

She looked frightened by it. Drew away from it.

I grabbed the receiver. Listened.

Disguised voice. No sex. No accent. No identifiable intonation.

"The old blacksmith barn, McCain. Check it out."

And hung up.

"Who was that?"

"Somebody who's seen a lot of mystery movies."

"What?"

"He or she wants me to check out an old barn on the east edge of town. By the old dam."

"Did the person say why?"

"That's rule number one in mystery movies: Anonymous calls should always be as mysterious as possible."

She stubbed out her cigarette. "Did you ever think somebody might just be having fun?"

"Not after midnight. After midnight you have to get a city permit to fool me."

She said, "Damn."

"What?"

She pointed at her head. "Depression."

"About what?"

"Depression and guilt, actually. The killer combo. My brother's not two days dead, and here I am in somebody's bed. And having a great time."

I stood up and pulled my shirt from the chair where I'd draped it. "C'mon. Depression has a hard time with moving targets."

"We're going to the old barn?"

"Thought we might."

"You're crazy, you know that?" she said.

"Yeah. But at least I'm not depressed."

IN LEGEND, THE first blacksmith in these parts was a Plains Indian said to have mystical powers. It was a nice story, but according to town records the first blacksmith was a guy named Louis J. Nordberg, Jr., who later ran for mayor. If he had mystical powers he kept them to himself. Yet whenever there was a town pageant of any kind, they dragged in this Indian named Night Star, who banged away at his anvil and spoke to ghosts. I guess it was better than Louis J. Nordberg, Jr., at that.

When I was growing up, the blacksmith barn was used for

livestock auctions. A couple hundred pickup trucks could be seen surrounding the pens twice a month, and an auctioneer who talked so fast I couldn't understand him strolled around in Western clothes and white Stetson, tilting his microphone like a crooner on Ed Sullivan.

Now it was a huge cattle barn laid out with bleachers and a show pen. The wood had begun to rot, and the smell of decaying timber combined with ghostly traces of dung to create a definitely unwelcome odor. You could still hear the sad, confused animals and the whine of Hank Williams played over the loudspeaker if you were attuned to the paranormal radio station that sometimes plays in my mind.

There were a number of STAY OUT signs posted. The doors were all padlocked sturdily.

"You bring a gun?" Natalie said, clutching my arm, shivering as much because of the creepy barn as because of the chill. There was even some ground fog rolling in. Pretty soon we'd have ourselves a drive-in horror movie.

"No."

"Why not?"

"Because if I bring a gun, somebody's likely to get shot."

"I thought all private eyes carried guns."

"Only the ones in the private eye union. I don't have enough money to join."

There was a boarded-up window that kids had pried open. The board came loose the moment I touched it. This told me that the kids of Black River Falls are as indomitable as ever, God love them. Crawl in and out of the barn but always put the board back in place so that it looks closed up. And people wondered where our future political leaders were coming from.

Inside, the wet-timber old-cow-dung smell was even worse. It had the same suffocating effect of being in a small closet filled with mothballs.

I'll spare you the tour we took. Nothing. The smells got worse. She clutched my arm tighter. We kissed a couple of times. And then I excused myself to do something people rarely do in mysteries when they're single-mindedly looking for clues: I stopped to take a leak. That's something you don't see very much of in Agatha Christie.

When we resumed our nothing search, I remembered the auctioneer's booth up in the corner. It was like the broadcaster's booth at a stadium. The auctioneer sat up there with his Pepsi and his Pall Malls and commented on all the beautiful animals being led into the pen.

The booth itself was the size of a prison cell. The auctioneer sat on one of three folding chairs at a booth-long counter for his microphone and made his announcements. On the wall, a ten-year-old poster announced the fact that on June 30, 1949, Mr. Roy Rogers and his horse Trigger would be appearing right here for the delight and wonderment of the entire family. I remembered that afternoon. I'd had a hell of a time until Trigger had a herculean bowel movement just when Roy was making him show off a little. That's the nice thing movies have over reality; you can always do another take. Most of our lives are in dire need of another take.

The booth had been used recently. Natalie pointed out a Pepsi bottle with the new Pepsi logo; I pointed out Cavalier cigarette butts in an ancient ashtray. The tobacco was still fresh. And then, as I played my light over the wall, we both saw it: blood spatters.

Richard Conners staggering out of the foggy night, not knowing where he'd been the past forty-eight hours. A head wound of some kind, blood all over his scalp.

A crime scene. That's what we were looking at. A man had been kidnapped and brought here. But why? I was able to answer that question a few minutes later when, crawling around on the floor with my flashlight, I saw a small plastic cap. I wasn't sure what it was. I showed it to Natalie.

"That's the protective cap they put on a hypodermic needle."

I'd handled it as carefully as possible, so as to get no prints on it. I wrapped it carefully in my handkerchief and put it in the pocket of my jacket.

"That's funny," she said.

"What is?"

"The hypodermic needle. In the stuff your police chief gave back to me—of my brother's, I mean—there was a small bottle of some kind of chemical."

Conners's missing forty-eight hours was starting to take shape.

"Let's take a look at that bottle."

"That's what I was thinking," she said.

On the way back to town, she lit a cigarette and asked if I'd turn up the radio. "Save the Last Dance for Me" was on.

"That's how I want my life to end," she said.

"How?"

"Dancing in the arms of my one true love and then sort of just fading up to heaven. You know, the way June Allyson and Van Johnson would in a musical." She paused. "The last dance. The very last dance. Russian girls are romantic. That's one thing not even the communists could take away from us."

"Not that they didn't try."

"Oh, yes," she said sadly. "Not that they didn't try."

A SQUAD CAR was parked outside the motel office. I could see the one and only Deputy Roger Weed inside, talking to the desk clerk. The clerk looked nervous. Roger just looked stupid. It was an expression he'd mastered. Roger had his notebook out and was writing in it with a ballpoint he had to keep shak-

ing to get ink. I half expected him to take out his police re-
volver and shoot it for loitering.

"I wonder what's going on," Natalie said.

"Hopefully, nothing that involves us. Let's go to your
room."

She was at the end. Several cars had red-white-and-blue
NIXON bumper stickers. He'd spent a lot of time in the state
lately. The next presidential race, in 1960, would probably be
Nixon versus Hubert Humphrey. The only possible dark horse
was Lyndon Johnson from Texas. It would be a pretty boring
election.

We parked and went to the door. Somebody was moving
around inside. I shushed her and pushed her gently away. I
wasn't sure what kind of reception I'd be getting when I
knocked.

I was thinking how lonesome my Smith & Wesson must be,
sitting at home night after night. I hadn't been kidding Natalie.
I left it home because just about every time I took it along,
somebody got shot. Fortunately, so far it hadn't been me.

I was just about to knock when the door opened.

He said, "What the hell you doing here, McCain?"

His name was Chilly Swacka, another one of Cliffie's min-
ions. He was different from the others because his IQ exceeded
his age and he was taking police courses at the U of I. He was
the night deputy, all dry-cleaned khaki uniform, Zachary Scott
mustache, and too-knowing eyes.

"The room belongs to a friend of mine," I said.

"Yeah? Who?"

Natalie stepped forward. "Me."

Swacka was suitably impressed. He got his nickname, by the
way, from jumping bare-ass naked into the river on a dare one
February morning when he was a kid. "Very pretty."

"Thank you," I said.

"He always this funny?" Swacka said.

"Twenty-four hours a day." Then, trying to look behind, around, and through him: "What happened in this room, officer?"

"Somebody tossed it. And the man in the room next door heard all the commotion and called the desk. Any idea what they might be looking for?"

"No."

I was beginning to wish I'd copyrighted the word *tossed*. It sure was getting a workout.

"You can look around if you want." He stepped back and let her pass. I heard her moan when she got inside.

I took out my Luckies and offered him one. He took it. It was one of those little gems that come along every once in a while. You smoke and they start to blunt your taste and you know that the only reason you're smoking is addiction and habit. But then every once in a while one of them will taste so good you remember why you started smoking. I try to remember that, every time the doctor has me get a chest X-ray.

Trucks on the highway. Cold wind from the river. Nat "King" Cole singing low and melancholy on a radio. Natalie letting go with little bursts of emotional pain every minute or so.

"That would tend to piss a guy off," Swacka said.

"Somebody going through your stuff like that?"

"Damned right."

He was ready to lead a manhunt. But I was fading. I wanted bed. Pamela came to me for a moment. She blew me a kiss. Tonight Natalie would be in bed with me instead, and that, I told myself, was fine with me.

She came out and said, "C'mon, McCain. Take me away from here. I just want to walk away and never see it again."

Then she was crying, probably from the same exhaustion

E D G O R M A N

that was beginning to hobble me. She slid her arm around my waist and tried to move me toward the ragtop.

"I have to finish up my report," Swacka said. "No sense you two staying."

"Thank you, officer," she said. "I appreciate your professionalism and courtesy."

Oh, he was dazzled all right. She could do that to you.

"My pleasure, miss," he said, all shy shit-eating grin. "My pleasure, you bet."

WE SLEPT. SHE was a good sleeper. She knew how to wrap herself around me without killing the circulation in any part of my body. Her hair smelled sweet and her flesh was warm and smooth. The cats liked her. When she got comfortable, they pressed themselves to her and got comfortable, too. Just an All-American family, we were.

THE SOUND OF the shower woke me. She was apparently an early riser. And a singer. It was a Broadway musical song. I had my first cigarette lying on my back, Tasha lying on my stomach. Natalie had a pot of coffee going. It smelled as good as coffee does on a chilly morning camping trip.

I got the radio on and am happy to report they were playing some Elvis from his Sun Records years. That's still the best Elvis, you ask me. They did what they called a "double-decker," two songs by the same cat. So we got "You're a Heartbreaker" and "Mystery Train," which may just be the best thing he's ever recorded.

And then came the knock.

Natalie, apparently accustomed to long leisurely showers,

was not troubled because she too was doing a double-decker. one from *My Fair Lady* and one from *The Music Man*.

I got a robe on and went to the door.

Raymond Chandler always says that any time he gets stuck in a story, he just has somebody come through the door with a gun in his hand. In this case, it was a her, the fetching young Negro woman Margo Lane. The gun looked wicked. Something the Germans came up with, no doubt. She carried a gray suede purse you could hide a Cadillac in. At first I didn't remember her. But then I remembered the aftermath of Conners falling dead in my office and me going out to the college where he taught. She'd introduced herself as one of his students. Now I knew better.

"You bastard," she said, marching me backward into my own apartment.

"And nice to see you again too, Margo," I said, not forgetting my duties as host. She wore a gray suit with gray suede pumps and white gloves. Even the reds had gone the white glove route. Lenin would not have been happy.

"Why'd you toss my room last night?" she demanded.

"Your room was tossed too? Somebody was busier than hell."

"Yes, and I know who it was: you."

"Why would I toss your room?"

We were being treated to a belted-out rendition of "On the Street Where You Live."

"Who's that?" she said.

"Just a friend."

"For a squirt, you sure seem to have a lot of 'friends.' "

"Thank you, and by the way, I really hate the word *squirt*."

"You do? Tough shit. Now tell me what you were looking for."

"You're mad but you don't even know what I was looking for? This is crazy."

"I just want to know if you know."

"Know what?"

She studied me and didn't seem especially pleased with what she learned. "Maybe you really *don't* know."

"What don't I know?"

The singing stopped and the bathroom door opened. Natalie came out in a white terry-cloth robe with a white terry-cloth towel wrapped turban-style around her head and said, "Oh, shit."

"Natalie? What the hell are you doing here?" Margo Lane said.

Natalie made an enigmatic but cute face and sighed. "The same thing you are, I suppose."

"You slept with the squirt here?" Margo asked, smirking.

"Don't be so smug, Margo. Do I have to remind you about Cleveland and that three-hundred-pound meat packer *you* spent a weekend with?"

Margo laughed. "All in the name of duty. You ever going to let me forget about that?"

"I will, if you don't ever tell anybody about this one. No offense, McCain."

Who were they? What the hell were they talking about? I knew I'd been insulted, but I was too confused to feel its sting.

Natalie helped herself to my cigarettes.

"I could use one of those," Margo said.

Natalie lit another one and took it over to her.

"Sit down, Margo," Natalie said. "I'll get us some coffee."

"So how was the shrimp?" Margo said as Natalie poured.

"Not as bad as you might think."

Not exactly a tribute.

"I ended up with a farm boy the other night," Margo said.

"He kept rubbing my skin. Like it was going to come off on his fingers or something."

Natalie poured two cups, carried them on saucers over to the small table, and sat down. I obviously wasn't invited.

Natalie said, "Why don't you go take a shower, McCain? We need to talk."

"If she's a communist," I said to Natalie, "who the hell are you?"

"You really *haven't* figured it out yet, have you?" Margo Lane said scornfully. "Man, you plow jockeys need to get a full deck of cards before you sit down to play with us city slickers. She's America First, you dumb shit."

"What?"

You know how in spy novels the beautiful woman who turns out to be a foreign agent weeps and begs for forgiveness right before our hero is forced to shoot her? Well, I was just about to pour myself a cup of coffee when Natalie said, "There isn't that much coffee to go around, McCain. I'd appreciate it if you'd just leave it for us and go take your shower."

"I can't have my own coffee?"

"How can you take his whining?" Margo Lane said to Natalie. "It'd drive me bat shit."

"It *does*," Natalie said.

My ego couldn't take anymore. I headed for the shower. But at the last minute, I turned and said, "Was he actually your brother, Natalie?"

Natalie smiled. Margo exploded. "Boy, you really *are* slow. Of course he wasn't her brother. He was just this mad dog anticommunist who fucked up the whole assignment and got himself killed."

"And just for the sake of squirts and dumb shits everywhere, what was the assignment?"

Natalie sipped her coffee—correction: my coffee—and said,

"Think about it, McCain. Rivers and Cronin kidnap Conners and take him to that old show barn. We find a cap for a hypodermic needle there."

"Sodium Pentothal," I said. "They injected him with it. Truth serum."

"Highly exaggerated track record," Margo Lane said. "It works about twenty percent of the time. It makes some people so psychotic it scrambles everything they say. They start to hallucinate—and that's what they tell you about. Not the information you're after but the fact that in their minds these purple guys from Venus are chasing them. And some people lie under the influence. They've lied so much about their lives the serum can't unmask the lie."

"So," Natalie said, "you have to be very careful about the information you get. You have to be able to put it in the context of the person you're dealing with." She smiled at Margo. "Remember that chemistry professor in LA who convinced us he'd created this elixir that would let people live for three hundred years?"

"What a wasted month that was," Margo said.

"I don't understand," I said, looking at both of them sitting there, all friendly and everything. "If you're on one side and she's on the other, why're you working together?"

"Oh, we're not working together at all," Natalie said. "If I had to, I'd kill old Margo here in a minute. And she'd kill me even faster. But we always get the 'girl' assignments. So since we're together so much, why not have a friendly rivalry?"

"What did Cronin get from Conners, a confession?"

"Supposedly they made a tape. Supposedly, Conners talks about his links to the communists," Natalie said. "That's why we want to get our hands on it. I want any names and dates and places he might have given. We'll use it to destroy his reputation, show that one more liberal icon really was a communist."

"And we want the tape to destroy it," Margo said. "We have a lot of agents in place in this country. A tape by Conners could expose them all."

"So where do you look for this tape?"

"Well, with Rivers dead, that leaves only Cronin," Natalie said. "I was hoping you could lead me to him. That's why I was hanging around. But—no luck."

"We have to find Cronin," Margo said.

"You two scare the shit out of me," I said.

Natalie giggled and Margo laughed. "Good," Margo said.

I WAS JUST drying off in the bathroom when the phone rang. I opened the door. Natalie and Margo were gone. No surprise there.

I got the phone on the fifth ring.

"You need a butler," Judge Whitney said.

"Now there's a practical idea," I said.

"Did you see the Channel Three news last night?"

"Afraid I missed it."

"Well, two of my friends were downstairs and happened to be watching television. And afterward they said they had no idea this kind of 'witch hunt' was going on out here."

"I'll bet the poor dears were so distressed they choked on their caviar."

"You base your whole idea of rich people on those idiotic Three Stooges movies you watch on TV. Caviar isn't nearly as fashionable as it once was."

"I'll bet the fish are glad to hear that."

"So what're you doing about all this, McCain? I'd planned

a nice bucolic week for my friends, and now all they'll talk about is how the scare is still going on out here. It's embarrassing."

"Actually, I'm working on it."

"That's what you always say when you're stumped. From what I hear, you're spending most of your time squiring that young Russian girl around town."

"Not anymore."

"What does that mean?"

I sighed. "Never mind."

"Well, get this thing over with, will you? My God, isn't it enough that I have to live here? Do I have to *defend* these people too?"

"I'll call you later today, Judge."

She clicked off.

TWELVE

Sometimes you just need to slow down. So much happens to you so quickly, you can't make any emotional sense of it. Take the commie and the anti-commie. Deadly enemies, one would suppose, and Natalie *had* assured me she'd be delighted to kill Margo if need be, but there they were swapping jokes about the various questionable lays they'd endured ("Not as bad as you might think" leaving a lot to be desired in the Ringing Endorsement Department) and speculating together on how best to conduct the case they were on. Joe McCarthy would be seriously pissed if he'd been alive to hear this.

I drove to the office with the top down. It was a ridiculously gorgeous day of squirrels lugging nuts to hiding places, piles of burning leaves sending intoxicating aromas into the air, and sweet-faced middle-aged women looking good in jeans and flannel shirts and work gloves raking the hell out of their lawns. There's a certain type of middle-aged bottom that I've come to appreciate in my dotage.

First place I went was my office. Probably several hundred thousand dollars' worth of checks waiting there for me and a note from the tax people saying that because I was such a wonderful guy I wouldn't have to pay tax on a penny of it.

There weren't any checks. On the other hand, there weren't any bills either. I made some phone calls, did some paperwork, and then decided I needed a milkshake and a paperback crime novel. I was running low on Harry Whittingtons.

The walk to Rexall was pleasant indeed. I visited with Old Lady Spritzer, Old Man Doggins, Father O'Malley, Coach Wylie, Fire Chief Bradford, Principal McCune, and the leader of our town's first and only rock-and-roll band, Ronnie "No Chin" Hanes. The nickname pretty much explains itself. He's tried for years to get folks to call him "the Seminole" because he insists he's 1/158th Indian or something like that, but "No Chin" seems to have stuck.

Every conversation went the same way: starting out with the weather, then talking about the good harvest the farmers were having, and then puzzling aloud as to who could've killed Conners and Rivers, and just where the heck was Jeff Cronin anyway, his wife and kids worried sick?

The Rexall lunch hour was winding down. There was a line at the cash register paying for ham sandwiches and hamburgers and chocolate cake, but there was only one person at the counter, Bob Steinem, who manages the A&P. He reads science fiction the way I read crime. What he was reading this lunch break was an Ace Double Book called *Lest We Forget Thee, Earth* by somebody named Calvin M. Knox. I couldn't see what the book on the flip side was.

Mary Travers gave me a glass of water and a weary smile. She wore a blue crew-neck sweater with a crisp white Peter Pan collar and a gray knee-length skirt. In her hair was a sweet little baby-blue barrette. "I hear you've been busy, Sam."

Mary is the girl everybody says I should marry. And they're probably right. Speaking in strictly superficial terms, she's as good-looking in her dark-haired way as Pamela is in her golden-haired way. And speaking in terms a little more meaningful—though I can be as superficial as the best of them, and don't let anybody tell you different—she was the smartest girl in our class and would've gone on to college but her dad got throat cancer the year we graduated high school, and her mom already had a long list of pretty serious ailments, so Mary stayed home to take care of them. These days, she was engaged to Wes Lindstrom, a pharmacist and son of the man who owned this Rexall. She doesn't love him and she knows it, and I know it, and I reckon Wes knows it too. I'd feel sorry for him if he wasn't such an imperious, judgmental jerk. He always reminds her what a big favor he's doing her by taking her out of the Knolls and building her a house on the "respectable" side of town. Aw, hell, I *do* feel sorry for him. You marry somebody and you have the right to expect them to love you to the same degree, or at least not to have anybody else in their heart. But she loves me and I love Pamela, though I love Mary too in some inexplicable way. It's sexual—she really is a quietly sexual girl—but there's something so fundamentally good about her that sometimes I can just stand there and watch her and feel this horny sorrow and respect lash me to her. Then I can't keep my hands off her. Which is why I stay away. I've hurt her too much already. I don't owe it to her to love her—anymore than Pamela owes it to me to love me—but I have an obligation not to deceive her.

"Yeah, very busy," I said. "You know, keeping the world safe for democracy."

She grinned. She's got one of those surprised-and-delighted young-girl grins. And I love to make it happen. I play her face the way I do a pinball machine. But instead of racking up points I try to rack up smiles.

"Oh, yes, I feel much safer, now that I know you're watching out for us."

"How're the malts today?"

"Good as always."

She didn't have to ask. Pineapple malt was my regular. Maybe I can't hold liquor because of my size, but you should see me pour down the malted milks.

She set my malt down and said, "Wes and I are going to take a little break."

"What?"

She nodded. "Same old thing."

Think things through about us. "Gee, I never see you except in here."

"He just can't get us out of his head. No matter what I say."

"Oh, hell, he'll come back, Mary."

She started wiping the counter with long, lovely hands. "You remember when you were little and you just knew that some-day everything would make sense to you and everything would be fine?'

I smiled. "Sure."

"When's that day going to come, Sam?"

"I don't happen to know personally, but I'm sure Kookie does."

The kid grin. "You still hate him, huh?"

"Yeah; yeah, I really do."

Are there TV and movie stars who really bug you? I mean, on a personal level? They just irritate you so much you want to back over them with a dump truck? Edd "Kookie" Byrnes, the boy sexpot of the otherwise enjoyable detective show 77 *Sunset Strip*, had that effect on me. Every time he came on, I wanted to take my gun out and start blasting away.

Bob Steinem stood up, left a tip for Mary, and said, "Don't

worry, McCain. I hate him too. Every time I see his face I want to punch it."

"Do I detect some jealousy here?" Mary said innocently. "Or maybe even some intimidation?"

"That jerk doesn't intimidate me any," Steinem said, as he walked to the cash register, "and I'm sure he doesn't intimidate McCain here, either."

After she'd cleaned up Steinem's dishes, she said, "Any idea yet who killed Conners and what's-his-name? Rivers?"

"Not yet."

"And no word on Cronin?"

"Nobody's seen him." Then I started talking about it. From the beginning, I mean. Everything. From the day we went to see Khrushchev to this morning, when it turned out that Natalie wasn't Rivers's sister at all but one of his fellow operatives. I told her about Margo, too.

"She had lunch in here yesterday. Really beautiful woman. Nice and friendly."

"She would be," I said. "To her you're one of the exploited masses."

"I feel like that sometimes." Then: "You ever consider that either Margo or Natalie might have killed them?"

"Why would Margo kill Conners? He was on her side."

"Maybe he was dangerous to her side all of sudden."

"Dangerous how?"

"Maybe he was going to talk to the FBI or HUAC. People have been doing that a lot lately."

And they had: professors and scientists and actors worried that their time as thirties leftists might get them in trouble someday. Better to go to Washington and tell your tale—and name names—than have the House Un-American Activities Committee come after you.

"And Natalie would kill him—why?"

"The opposite reason. He wouldn't come through for her. He had something she wanted—information—but he wouldn't let her have it. You sleep with her, Sam?" she asked suddenly. "No, no, don't tell me. I know you did, but if you say so it'll just make me feel worse." She went back to speculating. "Maybe Rivers got his hands on it, whatever it was, and that's why he was killed."

"I can see why *Margo* would kill him. But not Natalie."

"Maybe Natalie and Rivers had a falling out of some kind. Or maybe she wanted the credit all to herself."

"You're fishing now."

"I can only be brilliant so long."

"But I like your idea about one of them being the killer. They have the only real vested interest."

She shook her head. "I feel sorry for poor Dana. She was so proud of Richard."

"I suppose she had reason to be. I didn't always agree with his politics, but he had a pretty amazing career."

She made a face. "He wasn't much of a husband."

"Why do you say that?"

She took a box of straws and started refilling the plastic cylinder on the counter. "He was in here late one night and asked me if I wanted to have a drink with him. I thought he'd be interesting, and I was flattered. We had a few drinks over at Tilly's and then he gave me a ride home. He nearly raped me."

The story seemed illogical at first. You marry a lovely woman thirty years your junior and you run around? Didn't make any sense. But with his grand ego and ambition, conquest was probably his forte. He'd had the young and lovely woman at home. Now it was on to other conquests.

"Did you tell anybody?"

"When Mom died last year, Dana sent me a little essay she'd

read on mourning. It really helped. And I'd never even met her formally. It was just so thoughtful. I'd misjudged her. She gives the impression of being a very cold, arrogant woman, but she isn't at all. She even called me a few days later to see how I was doing."

"He ever bother you again?"

"No. The few times I saw him afterward, he had the good grace to look embarrassed."

Three young women came in from the shops down the block. They lit cigarettes and giggled and parked their nice trim bottoms on the upholstered counter stools.

At the register, as I was paying my bill, Mary said, "There's a Robert Ryan picture at the drive-in tonight."

She knew the way to my heart, sweet Mary did.

I WENT INTO Leopold Bloom's only when it was absolutely necessary. Stephen and Eileen Renauld had gone to the university in Iowa City, where they learned how to speak French well enough to impress yokels, and to write and compose and paint and sculpt so well that they were beyond sharing their work with the public. The public, coarse philistines, could never properly appreciate such beauty. So instead they ran one of those little bookstores where you suffocate in all the good taste: Persian rugs, Debussy on the record player, and every picture of James Joyce ever taken except maybe for the rectal X-ray he had in later years. Oh, and you also got their opinions on what was All Right to read and what Was Not. Those who can't, teach, is true enough—and they also own bookstores.

Fortunately, the Renaulds must have been off saying their daily prayers to D. H. Lawrence. They weren't in the shop. One of the local beatniks was, a skinny girl in pigtails with a beret. "I'm afraid we don't sell your kind of books in here," she said with practiced disdain. Apparently, the Renaulds kept a list of people who didn't belong there.

"Don't worry," I said. "I won't touch anything and contaminate it."

"I just meant I know what kind of books you read. Those—paperback things."

Having once made the mistake of special ordering *The Collected Stories of Erskine Caldwell* in here, I'd been a marked man ever since. But I figured if Caldwell was good enough for old Bill Faulkner, he was probably good enough for old Sam McCain. I didn't bother to point this out. This was their store and they were the unchallenged king and queen of all they surveyed.

I'd come in today because I saw Bill and Chris Tomlin through the window. I went back to them now. They were in the nonfiction section.

Chris wore sunglasses that looked especially dark and imposing against her pale medieval-virgin skin and short red hair. I wondered what the shades were all about. True, it was sunny outdoors, but inside here it was rather dark and a mite chilly. She wore a white sweater beneath a blue jumper. The supple body wasn't lost in the shapelessness of the garment, nor was the erotic face in the odd cant of her head. The angle looked uncomfortable. I wondered if she'd hurt her neck.

I said, "I wanted to see how things were going out at the Conners house."

Tomlin shrugged. He wore his usual European-cut suit. This one was double-breasted and blue and had traces of cigarette ash on one of the pockets. He was always mussed up somehow. A good thing he was so clearheaded when it came to organizing and chronicling the life of Richard Conners. The aging altar-boy face, the graying dishwater-blond hair, and the one blue walleye made me feel sorry for him as usual.

"Still in shock, pretty much," he said, in his quiet, southern-tinged voice. "Dorothy stares out the window. And Dana goes on her rampages"—he nodded to his wife—"that's why she's wearing the sunglasses."

"I didn't want you to think I'd gone Hollywood," she said.

"Dana gave Chris a black eye the other night. Made some stupid accusation and just started hitting her."

I was going to ask her about the accusation but just then the girl came by. "Could you please be a little quieter? This is a bookstore. There's a very nice café right down the street."

"We need to be going anyway," Chris said.

"There's a lot of work to be done now," Tomlin said. "Finish the biography. Harvard wants his papers. I have to start organizing them."

The girl came around to scowl at us again. We couldn't be disturbing the customers because there weren't any customers. Probably my mere presence in the store disturbed her.

We went outside and stood in the grace of the beautiful day.

He said, "Any word on Jeff Cronin yet?"

"No."

"That's the damnedest thing. Him not showing up at the school board meeting last night and then going missing."

"You think he's dead, McCain?" Chris said.

"I don't know."

"Neither does Cliffie," Tomlin said. "God, he's such a clown." He looked at his watch. "Well, we'd better go."

When they were half a block away, I realized I'd forgotten to ask them exactly why Dana would attack Chris. Then I thought again of the day when we'd gone to see Khrushchev, and the argument I'd seen between them.

I was standing on the corner, wondering what to do next, when a gentle voice said, "You look lost."

She'd changed into a crisp red blouse and black skirt and hose and black flats. The skirt was cinched by an outsize patent leather belt. Quite high-fashion for our little burg. She carried a small paper shopping bag. Men of every age paused to gawk at her. She was eminently gawkable, let me tell you, this dark-haired girl-woman with her big-city elegance out here on the prairie. She held up the shopping bag. "I like to pick up souvenirs whenever I can."

"I didn't know spies did stuff like that. Sounds pretty mundane."

"First of all, I'm not a spy. I just work for the foundation."

"Ah."

"And second, of course spies do stuff like this. They're human too."

"You couldn't prove it by me."

"Spies are necessary."

"I suppose."

"You don't even like the spies on your own side?"

"All the lies you have to tell. All the innocent people you have to hurt." Then I said, "Say, all that Russian junk you told me. I know Rivers wasn't your brother, but were you really born in Russia?"

"New Haven, Connecticut." She touched my arm again. "Poor McCain. It's just not a very nice world, is it?"

The Best Part of Going to the Movies
by Sam McCain

1. Coming attractions
2. Popcorn
3. Good 'n' Plentys
4. Milk Duds

This is when you go to a downtown theater. You know, indoors. The list changes considerably when you go to the drive-in.

The Best Part of Going to the Drive-in
by Sam McCain

1. Home run in the back seat
2. Third base
3. Second base
4. First base
5. Coming attractions
6. Popcorn
7. Good 'n' Plentys
8. Milk Duds

I know I should use more sophisticated language here—I mean, first base and second base sound kind of dopey for a twenty-five-year-old—but it gets the point across.

The best time for the drive-in is the summer: Buck Night, the whole carload for $1, when you hide people in the trunk; Rock Night, when all the local bands take turns playing on the concession roof and you vote by honking; and Fright Night, when people dress up. But summer was past now.

We both dressed warm and got a car heater, too. We rolled the window up on the driver's side so that the only opening was where the cord from the speaker went. The drive-in was only about half full. The shows started early these days because dusk came right at dinnertime. The Robert Ryan flick was called *Inferno*. I'd seen it several times before, but I found new things in it every time. Ryan's wife and her lover leave Ryan to die in the desert and he has to make it back to civilization. I like Ryan because he's the only one of the tough-guy leading men who shows you his suffering. I think that's why he's never been the big star he deserves to be. He lets you see the sorrow and the confusion and the panic. Most people would rather see some boring sonofabitch like Clark

Gable, who looks good even in a suit and talks like he knows all the answers.

Fortunately, *Inferno* was the only A flick on the triple bill tonight. You go to the drive-in because you can have sex, smoke cigarettes, drink beer, pee outdoors if you're in the back rows, and sit on the car hood and watch if you've had enough sex-cigarettes-and-beer for a while. And the movies should fit right in, too. The last two features were *High School Hellcats* and *Teenage Caveman*. Next week's triple "wham" feature was *Riot In Juvenile Prison, Girls On the Loose,* and *Dragstrip Girls*.

Halfway through *Inferno*, we were making out. I felt sorry for her and sorry for me. It was going to take a lot of lip-locking to make us feel good again.

Here goes McCain, he's rounding first and heading for second.

I hadn't kissed Mary in a long time. I'd forgotten how soft her flesh was. And how well she kissed. And how her breasts were just right: friendly but dignified. We steamed up the windows and then we were crawling into the back seat. Now we regretted dressing so warm. We had to take off both jackets and sweaters. We were high school hellcats, was what we were.

As I said, I don't talk much about my sex life, except with Maggie Yates, and I only talk with her because she says that having the kind of sex we have means absolutely nothing other than the fact that we're both horny. Maggie gets some kind of stipend from her New York fashion model sister, and this lets her keep writing her novel, which she claims is a combination of *Peyton Place* and *The Grapes of Wrath*. Your guess is as good as mine.

The thing with the car happened when I came up for air. We'd made it so warm that I was down to my T-shirt and I needed a break. It was becoming obvious that after all these years we were going to share a home run. I was ready and so was she. The noise the shocks were making was squeaky testament to our lust. And then, while I was kneeling on the seat next to Mary, who was shimmying out of her panties, I rubbed my hand against the steamy back window and saw it. Parked in the last row. At an angle you wouldn't choose unless the place was packed and you were forced to.

Jeff Cronin's black Studebaker, the futuristic-looking one.

"Wow," I said.

"Oh, no," she said. "Don't fink out on me now. I want this to happen, Sam."

"I know. So do I."

But we both knew I was seriously distracted.

"God, Sam, c'mon back down here."

"I just need to check it out."

"Oh, Sam. It isn't even that I'm so horny. It's just that it would *mean* something to me. It really would."

I lost it and she found it for me again and then we did it and it was great—but great as it was, the whole time we were thrashing around at least half my mind was on the black Studebaker. Cronin had been missing all this time. Now was he sitting at the drive-in watching a movie?

I held her afterward.

"If I start to tell you I love you, Sam, slap me, will you?"

"Upside the head or across the bottom?"

She laughed. "Both." Then she said, "God, I had this so built up in my head."

I couldn't help it. I kept staring out the back window I constantly wiped clear.

"It was going to be like a movie. And it'd be so wonderful for you, we'd be inseparable the rest of our lives."

I wrenched my gaze from the back window.

"I'm too crazy now with everything to say anything you

could rely on, Mary. But I love you. I don't even know what that means for us. Maybe I love you like a kid sister. Or maybe I love you just because you're such a good woman and I respect you so much. Or maybe I love you because of those wonderful breasts you have, or your bottom; that's very nice too. Or maybe all those reasons put together. Or maybe none of them. I mean, maybe I don't love you after all. Maybe love isn't the right word here. I just don't know. And I don't want to lead you on. But I want to start seeing you, I know that much. And I've never felt that before. So maybe that means something— or maybe it doesn't. Maybe it's just because—"

"Sam, will you shut up and go check out Cronin's car? That's what you want to do anyway, and you're starting to descend into gibberish, as Mrs. Fulton used to say." Mrs. Fulton was our tenth grade English teacher.

"Wait here," I said, pulling on my clothes. "I'll be right back."

She gave me a quick, lovely kiss. "You'd better."

There wasn't anybody in it. That was the first wrong thing. The second wrong thing was that the engine was running.

It took me a few minutes to find the third wrong thing. I took the key from the ignition and went around to the trunk and opened the lid and there he was.

I touched his forehead. It was colder than it had any reasonable right to be. And then I reached down for his wrist. It was as disappointing as all those signals we send into outer space. No response whatsoever.

PART III

THIRTEEN

Y OU KNOW, McCAIN, IF you're not real careful, people just might mistake you for an asshole."

Now, there are many things people accuse Cliffie Sykes Jr.
of—sloth, ignorance, duplicity, intolerance, smelling bad—but
wit is not one of them.

So I couldn't help but smile, even though the barb was aimed
at me.

"Cliffie," I said, "who's writing your material these days?
That's actually funny."

He shrugged. "Actually, I heard this state trooper say it to
some con he brought in. But I think of stuff like that all the
time."

Ah, the world made sense again. For a moment I'd worried
that it had gone off its orbit, Cliffie actually saying something
funny.

I should have been in a somber mood. Every man's death
diminishes me, and all that. But Jeff Cronin had been a special
case. He'd been bullying his way through life ever since he
reached kindergarten. And in the past few years, what with the

red scare and all, his bullying had taken an especially nasty turn.

The folks at the drive-in couldn't figure out which was more interesting, the juvenile delinquent movie on the screen or the real-life crime movie in the back lane. On the screen one juvie had stabbed another juvie to death and a couple of tough cops (whom I recognized from RKO Westerns)—were commenting on "youth run wild."

An ambulance, two police cars, four cops, Doc Novotny, and movie-goers-turned-gawkers now surrounded the black Studebaker. Cronin's body was still in the trunk. Only one of the cops had his uniform on. The others had been dragged from home and wore sweatshirts and jackets with large police badges in conspicuous places.

Cliffie went over my story twice. Then he said, "You're so smart, McCain, why would somebody put a stiff in the trunk and leave the motor running?"

"Panic."

"Huh?"

"Got scared. Thought maybe somebody spotted them. Ran off and left the key in the ignition."

He looked at me and shook his head. "My old man's on my ass."

"For what?"

"For what? For all the shit that's goin' on in this town. Personally, I think this place is crawlin' with commies."

"Black River Falls is crawlin' with commies?"

"You're damned right. I seen this movie on TV the other night, I Married a Communist, and that's the first kinda broad the Ruskies go for."

"What kinda broad we talking about?"

"You know, the teacher."

"Helen Toricelli."

"Hell, yes, Helen Toricelli. That's how the commies do it. They get these teachers to sneak in all this commie philosophy, and then before you know it your kids've turned red."

I'm sure he slept well, Cliffie. The world was such a simple, knowable place to him. Nothing to trouble his slumber.

"If you say so."

"So anyway, my old man says we need to find out who's been killin' all these people, because otherwise the state attorney general may send some investigator out here to start lookin' into things."

Cliff Sr. knew that Cliff Jr.'s police work would never stand up to any scrutiny. The press would love to get details of Cliffie's incompetence. It was one of those moments when I almost felt sorry for him.

"The Judge is on my ass, too."

"Oh, yeah? How come?"

We stood at the two-foot wooden fence that ran around the back of the drive-in. The night was colder now. You could see your breath. A plane roared overhead. A train hooted in the distance. It was a busy night on the prairie, and I couldn't get over how the movie crime scene compared to the real one in the back row.

"She's got some of her friends from back East here. She thinks all this red scare stuff makes us look ridiculous. Which it does."

He sighed. "Between us, the wife thinks Cronin got carried away. She lived next door to Helen Toricelli when she was growin' up. Helen used to baby-sit her. So when Jeff'd stop by and start talkin' about what a commie Helen was"—he paused—"he was a prick."

"Who was?"

"Jeff."

"I thought he was your friend."

"I probably shouldn't say this, with him still in the trunk and all, but he was a jerk. He had a nice little wife and he couldn't leave the other broads alone. He got around, that boy did. And he always had to let you know you weren't as smart as he was, either. He was drunk one night and he told me I didn't know shit from Shinola about police work. You believe that? After I took that correspondence course and everything?"

I tried to commiserate but I couldn't quite get the words out. Shit from Shinola might not have been eloquent, but it stated the truth.

"Hell, he was sniffin' around Tomlin's wife one night out at the softball park."

"Chris Tomlin? Why would she have anything to do with him?"

He shrugged. "You know how lover boys are. They just get the broads. Broads that shouldn't want to have nothin' to do with them."

A Ph.D. from Yale. A contributing editor to *Atlantic Monthly*. A woman who'd written three or four well-received books. And she was spending time with Jeff Cronin?

"I ain't sayin' anything actually happened."

"I can't believe it."

"But she was definitely interested in him. Up by the pavilion above the river there? Roger Weed had this bowling tourney over to Williamsburg that night, so I had to cover for him. That's when I seen 'em, Jeff and the Tomlin gal. Sittin' on a bench in that pavilion all by their lonesome."

One of his men started toward him. "Need you over here, Chief."

He said, "I don't want no inspector comin' in here tryin' to second-guess me, McCain. Make the whole town look bad."

And not only the town.

"So if you find out anything—"

"I'll tell you right away."

He clapped me on the shoulder. He'd never been friendly before. I wasn't sure I liked it. "I'll get the old man off my back and you'll get the judge off yours."

Then he walked away to play cop. Just the way his correspondence course had taught him to.

"SOMETIMES I HATE to go inside," Mary said. We were parked in front of her house in the Knolls. There was the darkness and the wind, enough wind to rock the ragtop.

"How come?"

"All the memories. You know, first Dad dying, then Mom."

"I'm sorry, Mary."

"I probably should sell it."

"Maybe you should."

"But I wouldn't get much."

"Maybe enough to pay down on a house somewhere else."

"That always looks so strange, though. A woman living alone in a house."

"Times are changing."

Then she said, "I don't suppose this is going to go anywhere, is it?" She looked straight out the window at the night, at the way the light pole swayed in the wind on the corner.

"You mean tonight?"

"Yes."

"I just don't know."

"God, I wish I could keep my mouth shut. Here a man dies and all I can think about is myself."

Moonlight didn't redeem the houses in the Knolls. If they looked bad in the daylight, they still looked bad in the moonlight. Busted windows, tarpaper patches on the exterior, front door ajar, a junk car or two on the front lawn. Every once in

a while you'd see an obstinately neat little house where everything was kept up. Mary's house was like that. My folks' house
in the Knolls had been like that too. We'd lived there physically
but not spiritually.

"I wonder if his wife knows yet."

"Cronin's?"

"Yes. She's nice."

"That's what Cliffie said. He also said that Cronin ran
around a lot."

"That's what I heard."

"You did?"

She nodded. "At the lunch counter I heard people talking
about Cronin and Chris Tomlin. I felt sorry for Mrs. Cronin.
She's at mass every day and always delivering food baskets to
the poor. I don't know why she ever married him." She
shrugged. "His looks, I guess. He was a good-looking man, I
have to give him that."

She leaned over and kissed me on the cheek.

"Don't worry, Sam, I'm not going to make anything of tonight. We'll just see what happens."

"I appreciate that."

" 'Night."

She started to open the door. I grabbed her and kissed her
the way she deserved and needed to be kissed. "I had a good
time tonight."

She smiled sadly. "Well, except for the murder."

"Yeah, I guess that part wasn't so good, was it?" I smiled
sadly right back.

She got out of the car and went into the small dark house.
I waited until a light went on inside and then pulled away.

*   *   *

OH, THEY WERE a jolly pair, they were. I wondered how long they'd been drinking. I didn't have to wonder about how they'd gotten through my back door. That was their profession, getting through front, back, and side doors and taking whatever they wanted in pursuit of the truth—or the truth as they happened to see it, anyway, the truth of the far right versus the truth of the far left.

Margo Lane and Natalie Rivers. Or whatever the hell their real names were.

At least they brought their own booze.

They sat at my small dining table smoking their cigarettes and sipping their J&B scotch. The record player was on: Elvis.

"Well, look who's here," Margo said.

"Our friend the private eye," Natalie said.

"I'll bet he's got some information he'd just love to share with us."

"I don't know." Natalie giggled. "He looks pretty dumb to me."

They *both* giggled, Margo in a black blouse with the slender gold necklace fetching against her dark skin; Natalie in a forest green sweater and one of those matching bands in her hair that college girls wear these days.

"You're running low on toilet paper," Natalie said.

"They're having a sale on it at the A&P," Margo said.

"Consider the social implications of running out of TP, McCain," Natalie said.

I went over and got myself a beer and sat down at the table with them.

"They found Cronin," I said.

"We know," Natalie said.

"It was on the news," Margo said.

"In the trunk of his car," Natalie said.

"At the drive-in," Margo said.

"Dead," Natalie said.

"With the ignition running," Natalie said.

"So why don't you tell us something we don't know?" Margo said.

"Gee," I said, "a couple of whiz kids like you two, I wouldn't think there was anything you I could tell you."

"We don't know *everything*, McCain," Margo said.

"But close to everything." Natalie smiled.

"Cliffie wants me to help him. Since this involves politics, Cliffie's old man is afraid the state attorney general'll send out his own investigators and expose Cliffie Junior for the dumb ass he really is."

"You going to help him?" Margo said.

"If it suits my purposes," I said. "What we're looking for is a tape. That's what this is all about."

"Maybe he isn't as dumb as he looks," Natalie said to Margo.

"Cronin and Rivers kidnap Conners. They shoot him up with Pentothal and make a tape recording of what he tells them while he's drugged. Then somebody kills Conners—and, very soon after, Rivers and Cronin."

"So who has the tape?" Natalie said.

"The killer," I said.

"And that would be who, exactly?"

"I don't know," I said.

"See," Margo said, "I told you he was as dumb as he looks."

"I'm afraid I have to agree with her on that one, McCain."
More giggling. It was like a slumber party.

"So the question now is, Who would *want* the tape?" I said. I watched them both. "And you know who I come up with?"

"Who?" Natalie said.

"Whom is proper in this case," Margo said.

"One of you," I said.

"One of us?" Margo said. "If one of us had the tape, why would we be here? Why wouldn't we be back at headquarters with our people, deciding how to use it?"

"I'd make copies," Natalie said, "and send one to every influential broadcaster in the United States. Richard Conners exposed as a communist in his own words."

"And I'd destroy it," Margo said. "Just because he gave away a few secrets doesn't make him a bad man. And anyway, he's very useful to us as a hero. Just the way McCarthy was for you folks, Natalie. You knew he was a bum, but for a long time your side got to use him as a hero. We may know that Conners really was a communist—but if that never gets out, we can go right on portraying him as an innocent who was picked on by you lunatics on the far right."

"It's why I love political extremes so much," I said. "Neither of you cares about the truth."

"I care about the truth," Natalie said, sipping scotch. "The truth is, he was a communist spy and should've been tried for treason."

"We don't know that for sure," I said. "Anyway, you want power, not truth. And so does Margo."

"Why would somebody want the tape if his confession isn't on it?" Margo said.

"That's what we need to find out," I said.

Natalie yawned. "I don't suppose you'd let me sleep here tonight, would you, McCain?"

"Probably not."

"God, are you still mad because I lied to you?"

"Gee, what kind of intemperate fool would I be if I got mad at everybody who lied to me?"

"It wasn't a big lie."

"Well, it sure as hell wasn't a *small* lie."

"Let's just say it was a medium-sized lie, all right? Don't be so hostile."

Margo said, "You want to get a pizza?"

Natalie looked at me. "Maybe McCain here'll change his mind and let me stay overnight."

"You'd be better off with a pizza. And so would I."

"He likes these small-town girls," Natalie said. She was starting to get belligerent.

Margo stood up and took her by the arm. "C'mon, you're drunk."

"Small-town girls for a small-time private eye."

Margo somehow got her to the back door. "She needs food."

Natalie got one last good glare off in my direction. "Small-town girls," she said. "Big fucking deal."

FOURTEEN

I spent the first working hour of my morning walking up and down the three long sunny blocks of retail shops on the west side of Main. I'd gone back to basics. Had anyone heard the gunshot? Had anyone seen or heard anything or anybody suspicious?

On my walk, watching some of the merchants sweeping the sidewalks in front of their stores, I had occasion to catch up on various items much on the minds of Americans these days. Mr. Potato Head seemed to be popular, as did Tiny Tears dolls; Spam claimed it tasted even better served with hot baked beans; the S&H redemption store had huge color photos of the molded plastic chairs and pole lamps and cloverleaf tables you could get when you collected enough of their trading stamps; and Fran's Fashion Frocks was running a special on tube dresses, sack dresses, and crinolines.

I saw the Princess Anne blouse on a mannequin as soon as I walked in and pictured how good it would look on Mary. I still felt uncertain about last night. If I'd taken advantage of her. If I hadn't simply—selfishly—made both of us more miserable.

"You know Mary Travers, don't you?" I asked Marge Downes, the owner (there had actually been a Fran of Fran's Fashion Frocks but she had shocked everybody and run away with the Lutheran minister).

"Sure, McCain. She shops here all the time." Marge is a Rosalind Russell kind of woman, trim and tall and given to severe business suits and ankle-strap shoes year round and large fashion hats that risked self-parody.

I pointed to the mannequin. "Would you have that in her size?"

"Let's step over here and look."

While she was looking through the blouses, I said, "Were you here the day Richard Conners was shot?"

She looked up at me. "I certainly was. I even heard the shot. It was loud enough that it had the women running out of the dressing rooms. Dana Conners—she was here with Dorothy Conners—was one of them. Of course, none of us knew what had happened. But my dad was a hunter. I know a gunshot when I hear one."

"You didn't see anybody on the street acting suspicious?"

"No. But then I wasn't looking on the street. A couple of the customers knew it was a gunshot, too, so they were very concerned." She held up a blouse. "Here we go. This is her size. She'd look very pretty in this." She peered at me from around the left shoulder. "When're you going to marry her, anyway? She's the prettiest girl in town. And neither of you is getting any younger."

There you had it. They talked like twenty-five was peering over the edge. That you had better by God get on with it. The trouble was, I didn't feel old. I wasn't a grown-up yet. I wanted to be, I tried to be, I apparently even occasionally gave the impression that I was. But I knew the truth: I wasn't. And as much as I wanted a wife and kids, the prospect scared me.

I smiled. "Maybe sooner than you think."

It took her five minutes to gift-wrap it. I walked down to the Rexall store. The soda counter was filled. You could get a good breakfast here for sixty cents, couple eggs, couple strips of bacon, couple pieces of toast. Mary looked at me and for just a moment—before the sweet, vulnerable smile—I saw the hesitation and confusion she was feeling. The same hesitation and confusion I was feeling. *Had last night changed everything? Was it the beginning of a new relationship or merely the end of the old one? What was the best move—or on her part or mine?*

She was busy pouring coffee and picking up orders from the grill. There wasn't time to talk. I held up the gift box and pointed from myself to her—*from me to you, Mary*—and then gave her a smile and left.

The next forty-five minutes, I spent working in and around the garage where Richard Conners had been murdered. It was a great morning to be outside. An aging gray tomcat accompanied me on my appointed rounds. He'd brush up against my leg and meow every once in a while. Other than that he seemed happy to be the first member of my feline private-eye club.

I talked to men who spent time in the alley, mostly warehouse guys who off-loaded merchandise trucks. None of them had heard the shot; none of them had seen anything or anyone untoward. They said the drunks who just *might* have seen something didn't start to appear until after dark, like vampires.

The Jag had been taken away. The garage was empty. I was walking it off, examining the floor for anything Cliffie might have missed, when Mr. Touchberry came up to me. "Couple boys in the back told me you were asking questions about the other day." In the early fifties, there was a popular TV show

called *Mr. Peepers*, about a small four-eyed Milquetoast
teacher who looked fussy and fey but turned out to be a pretty
good guy after all. That was Mr. Touchberry, Mr. Ralph
Touchberry. He was the manager and bookkeeper of Touchberry TV & Radio. His brother the salesman, Mr. Tom Touchberry, was a different type altogether. He squeezed your hand
into pulp when he shook it. He shouted when he spoke. And
he slapped your back so hard after one of his jokes, you had
to see a chiropractor.

"Yes," I said. "Did you hear the shot, Mr. Touchberry?"

Maybe he wouldn't have looked quite so much like Mr.
Peepers if he didn't wear those mix-and-max combo deals you
buy at J. C. Penney. You buy two sport jackets, one dark, one
light; and two pairs of trousers, one dark, one light—and then
you just keep mixing and matching. He had a couple of shirts
he rotated and maybe three bow ties. Even though he was well
into his forties, he always looked like a kid all dressed up for
his First Communion.

"No. But I was coming back from the Rexall—I always take
my morning break over there, that pretty Mary Travers is just
so darned nice—and I saw somebody coming out of the garage."

"This garage?"

"This very garage."

"Did you recognize him?"

"Of course. He bought a nice twenty-one-inch Admiral
home console from us just last month. Bill Tomlin."

I tried not to act excited. "You're sure it was him?"

"Of course. I mean, he kind of ducked back into the garage
so I wouldn't see him. But I saw him all right."

"Do you have any sense of what time this was?"

"My break is always from ten-thirty to ten-forty-five. It
never varies."

"That would make it around the time of the shot."

"The shot, I didn't hear. So there I can't help you. But I definitely saw Bill Tomlin in and around the garage that morning."

"Did you tell this to Cliffie?"

His little face made a little face. "I try not to talk to Cliffie unless it's absolutely necessary."

"I see."

"Have you ever heard of the Lawman's Discount?"

"No. I can't say as I have."

"Neither had I. But the day we got our very first color TV in—this really beautiful RCA nineteen-inch table model, and the color was just gorgeous, no green faces like the early ones—Cliffie comes in and says he'll take it. Well, naturally my brother Tom is all excited. We weren't sure how color TV would go over in Black River Falls, being so expensive and all. But we'd barely put the darn thing on the floor and Tom already sold it. Then Cliffie tells Tom that he—Cliffie—is entitled to the Lawman's Discount and Tom said he'd never *heard* of no Lawman's Discount and Cliffie said, Oh, yes, it was some kind of unwritten law, when a peace officer—that's what he likes to call himself, a peace officer, you know the way Matt Dillon does on *Gunsmoke*—he said that when a peace officer above the rank of captain goes to buy something, there's an unwritten law that he's entitled to a thirty percent discount. And Tom—well, I don't have to tell you about Tom and his temper—Tom just exploded and told Cliffie to get out. Which is when Tom started getting all these parking tickets. Old Cliffie paying him back." He smiled. "But at least we didn't give him any so-called Lawman's Discount." He shook his head. "So now I don't tell Cliffie anything I don't have to."

"Good. Can we keep this between us?"

"Sure. I'm not a talker, you know that." And he wasn't.

Then: "You ever want a deal on a TV, Sam, you go talk to Tom. He'll fix you up."

"Thanks, Ralph."

"Well, I better get back to my books. Payroll is this afternoon."

He gave a little wave and was gone.

AS I OPENED the door to my office a few minutes later, I heard the sounds of Jamie working merrily away at the typewriter. She must have been doing six or seven words a minute.

"Hi, Mr. C," she said, with her usual Teen Queen enthusiasm. "Bet you're surprised to see me here, huh? We had an inservice day at school so my dad said, You scoot your butt right down to Mr. C's office—well, actually, he doesn't call you Mr. C, he calls you Mr. McCain, I'm the one who calls you Mr. C. So here I am."

Lucky me.

"I've already typed this letter I found on your desk."

"Letter?" I said, going over to the coffeepot and setting it up for the day.

"If I drink coffee when I'm having my time of month, you know, I break out."

"Gosh," I said. "Imagine that."

"My whole family has crazy periods."

"Even your dad?"

She grinned. "Mr. C made a funny." She wore a simple blue skirt and tight buff blue blouse. She was cute and she was fetching and she drove me nuts.

I sat down at the desk and looked it over. On a large piece of white paper, she'd written *Shammus*.

"I'm not sure what this means, Jamie."

"What what means, Mr. C?"

"This note. Shammus."

"Oh, you know, like on TV."

"Like on TV?"

"Yeah, you know, what they always call a private eye. A shamm-us."

"That's shame-us."

"Oh, well, close enough. I just wrote it down so I'd remember to tell you that your pigeon lady called."

"My pigeon lady?"

"Yeah, shammuses have pigeons they go to, and the pigeons tell them stuff."

"That's stool pigeons." I was beginning to understand her, and the implication of that was frightening. We were doing George Burns and Gracie Allen here.

"Yeah. Close enough. Stool pigeons." She went back to her typing. Flying along with those two fingers. Then she blew a giant pink dome of bubble gum and said, "You ever notice how typing is hard on your fingernails, Mr. C?"

"Do you tell me who my stool pigeon is or do I guess? Could it be Helen Grady?"

"At the old folks' home?"

"Yes."

"Then that's her. You guess good."

"Does she want me to call her?"

"Uh-huh."

Another giant pink dome. "I'll have that letter for you in a minute."

I still didn't know what the hell letter she was talking about.

I called Helen Grady. The line was busy. I watched the coffee brew. I thought about calling Mary. I couldn't sort out my feelings. In some way, I loved her deeply. I just couldn't figure out which way that was and if it was the kind she needed. Or the kind I needed. Or—shit. Sometimes, I just want to reach up there and give myself a lobotomy. Life without thought would be so much easier.

I tried Helen Grady again. Still busy. I was jittery. I thought about the drive-in last night. Cronin. There was a possibility that Natalie or Margo had killed him. And killed Conners and Rivers, too. When I'd first met them, my ego had blinded me. These cute girls weren't harmless propagandists. I now believed they were quite capable of murder.

I tried Helen a third time. Still busy.

"Ouch," Jamie said. "Shit." Then: "Oh, fudge."

I'd been staring at the phone. When I looked up, I found Jamie at the coffeepot. She was shaking her hand. "Pardon my French, Mr. C, but I spilled hot coffee all over my hand and all over your letter."

"Are you all right?"

"I was going to surprise you, and now look." She seemed about to cry. "I ruined your coffee and I ruined your letter."

"It's all right, Jamie. Let me see the letter, will you?"

She brought it over. I read it. If she hadn't just burned her hand with the coffee, I probably would've swore. But I just said, "Well, we can worry about this letter later. There's some ointment in the cabinet over there. In a shoe box along with some Band-Aids. Go put some on."

"Gee, thanks."

What she'd done was taken a letter I'd scribbled off in longhand on February 2, 1957—more than two and a half years ago—and retyped it. Even though it was clearly rubber-stamped, in red, FILE COPY. I'd been looking at it in reviewing a current case. I solemnly promised myself never to leave another FILE COPY letter on my desk.

She came back and said, "I think maybe I need to rest this hand." She held it up the way she would a sick puppy.

"It looks pretty bad."

"Well, Turk said I have *nice* hands."

"Who's Turk?"

"My boyfriend this year."

"Ah, the 1959 model."

"Say again?"

"Never mind. I wasn't insulting your hands. You *do* have very nice hands. I just meant that it looks a little red where it was burned."

It didn't, of course. But I knew she was leading up to taking off the rest of the day, and I wanted to help her on her way.

"I think I may be running a fever, too."

"Those burns are fast acting."

"Maybe if I took the rest of the day off I could come charging back in here on Monday."

"A great idea."

"You're a peach, Mr. C."

I said, "You know, that's something I've always wondered about."

"What is?" She was even perkier now that she knew she'd soon be free and in the greasy clutches of a kid named Turk.

"My name is McCain but you always call me Mr. C."

"Oh, that," she said, as if explaining to a chimpanzee how to use a spoon. "It's because M and C are too hard to say. I mean, Mr. Mc doesn't sound right. So I dropped the M and just call you Mr. C because it's easier."

I sighed. "You're starting to look kind of pale, Jamie. If I were you I'd get out of here as fast as I could."

"Thanks for being so understanding, Mr. C."

And then, thank the Lord, she was gone.

I tried Helen Grady again, and this time I got through.

"Hello, doll," I said, in my best *Peter Gunn* voice.

"Hello, shamus. How's the gumshoe business?"

"Oh, not so bad. My trench coat needs a cleaning, though."

"I'll bet. All that blood." Then: "I've got a little free info if you're interested."

"Slather my ears with it, gorgeous."

"Seems there's this fishing cabin about two miles west of Ilten Basin. Owned by Bill Grant, the photographer? Well, he and Conners went way back. *Way* back. So Grant gave Conners a key to the cabin."

"I'm on the same streetcar you are so far, doll baby."

"Well, guess who used to bring his girlies out there? In particular, a certain Chris Tomlin?"

Chris Tomlin at a fishing cabin with Conners. Bill Tomlin in the garage just before Conners is killed. Does a shamus have to have somebody draw him a picture?

"Mind if I ask who's been giving you this inside dope?"

"You knows the Bransons?"

"Those strange folks who're always writing the paper about UFOs?"

"They live up there. And they're always sittin' on their front porch with binoculars lookin' for UFOs. So they see everything. And the mister, his mom's in the home here with me—"

"And they saw—"

"Several times they saw them together, gumshoe. Several times. You should maybe swing by there and give 'em the third degree. Watch out for Mrs. Branson, though."

"How come?"

A chuckle. "You'll find out."

THE TROUBLE WAS this: So Bill Tomlin kills Conners because Conners is sleeping with Chris. Fine. Happens all the time. But who killed Rivers and Cronin? Why would Tomlin kill *them*? Was Chris sleeping with them too? Unlikely. The life of a shamus is not an easy one.

On the way to the woods—dirt roads winding into sparkling autumnal wilderness—I had a Pamela attack. *God, how could she do this to me after all we'd meant to each other?* But only half the equation was true; *she'd* meant a lot to *me*. I loved her and hated her and wanted to protect her and wished her the absolute worst. And God did I miss her!

This particular leg of the river is about a mile from the dam. On a good day you can see all the way downstream to a large dock where the dance boat rests. A century ago, river boats up from the South plied these waters, docking with minstrels and dry goods. The one trouble with the area is the spring flooding, which is why, after a few major floods, the rich rebuilt on the bluffs about half a mile due east.

The Bransons had stayed behind. They were local legends. They lived in a little wooden shack that had first been condemned by the county in 1950. They also kept mongrel dogs they'd raised to kill. And the place was a health hazard. The last time they cleaned the interior was sometime around FDR's first inauguration. They'd had one child, a girl. One spring day, the Bransons had come to town in their clattering old pickup and driven straight to Doc Gibbons's office. The missus carried a large brown paper grocery sack in and set it on the receptionist's desk. The receptionist was busy on the phone at the time. The missus left the sack behind and walked back to the truck, and they headed home to their shack. A few minutes later the nurse opened the sack and found the body of a growth-stunted five-month old girl inside, filthy and naked. This was back in '50. I guess the Bransons figured that if old Doc Gibbons delivered her, they should bring her back to him when she died. Judge Whitney had wanted them charged with *some*thing—anything—but the Bransons were distant kin of the Sykes clan so all that was done was to condemn the shack. The little girl had died of natural causes, a kidney ailment. Living in a house filled with rats, dog feces, rotten food, and overflowing chamber pots probably hadn't helped her any, but it wasn't a death the county attorney could make a case of.

I saw a gag postcard once that read WELCOME TO OUR HILL-BILLY HOME. The drawing showed a grandpa hillbilly sitting in a rocking chair on the front porch of his tumbledown shack, a shotgun laid across his lap and a large collection of buxom beauties à la Daisy Mae in *Li'l Abner* surrounding him.

Well, with the Bransons, all you needed to do was put two rocking chairs on the porch—one his'n and one her'n—and instead of buxom beauties surround them with snarling, slavering, enraged dogs of every size and description. The shotgun? Make that *two* shotguns.

You know how I say I'm no hero? Well, I'm about to offer you absolute proof of this.

I didn't get out of the car. I pulled up so that my door faced their porch only ten feet away. No possibility I was going to get out.

The his'n and her'n motif kept right on going. They both wore bib overalls, blue T-shirts, and straw hats of the sort Huck Finn preferred. And one more thing—I swear this is true—they both had glass right eyes. Identical blue right eyes. And they both chewed tobacco. I could see why Helen Grady had warned me. He spat his tobacco into a Folger's coffee can next to his chair, but her tobacco went everywhere. She just lip-flung it wherever she felt like.

And then the mister, he performed a miracle of sorts.

Every one of the dogs was jumping up and down, barking, baying, growling, eager to leap from the porch, dive on my car,

tear off the doors, smash in the windows, and turn me into
another Spam creation for dinner.

But all he said—and not in a particularly loud voice—was
"Shut up!"

And they shut down. As if they were electronic and the
switch had been turned.

He hadn't even looked at them. He just said it.

An eerie silence settled upon us.

The only sound for two or three long minutes was her spitting tobacco in the general direction of my ragtop.

He said, "That's some fancy automobile."

"Yeah, I guess it is."

"You're that Sam McCain, ain't you?"

"Yes, I am."

"I had a boyfriend had a fancy automobile once," she said.

"Gosh," I said.

"She had a passel of boyfriends."

"I can sure see why."

" 'Course, she's put on a little weight since then."

That was another thing. Neither of them could've weighed
a hundred pounds. They looked emaciated. What did she used
to weigh, sixty?

"She carries it well," I said, just to keep things rolling.

The cabin looked to be one room, with tarpaper covering a
good deal of roof and exterior wall. The lone window was
boarded up with raw two-by-fours. The brick chimney was a
jumble. And the stench was ungodly, even from ten feet
away.

"Do somethin' fer you, mister?" she said. She couldn't de-
cide whether to look hostile or curious, so she settled for both.
She was as sinewy and tough-looking as her husband. They
could've been anywhere between forty and seventy. You just
couldn't tell. I couldn't, anyway.

"I'm working on the Conners case."

"That be Richard Conners?" he said. "The one who got hisself killed?"

I nodded.

The woman spat tobacco and then laughed. "He sure had a little one."

I wasn't sure I'd heard her correctly. "I beg your pardon?"

Husband said, "We used to watch him. Sneak up and peek through the window. They never did catch us. The wife here always made jokes about how little he was." He smiled. "She ever makes a crack like that about me, she'll be sportin' *two* glass eyes, I can tell ya that."

"No reason to say anything like that 'bout you, Rolly." She went on. "He got some lookers out to that cabin, though. I got to give him that."

"You ever see Chris Tomlin with him?"

"Did better than that," she said, and spat. "We seen Conners and the Tomlin gal inside the cabin—and then we seen Bill Tomlin, her old man, sneak up and peek in the window. We was back in the timber, watchin'."

"You sure it was Bill Tomlin?"

"Positive," Rolly said.

"We seen his pitcher in the paper," she said. "It was him, all right."

"Did he confront them?"

"What's that mean?"

"Did Tomlin start an argument with them or anything?"

"Nope," he said. "Just watched, then took off."

"And you saw him out there a couple of times?"

"Maybe even three," she said, and spat.

The smell was getting to me. And I figured the dogs would soon enough break out of their hypnotic spell and attack me.

All the chawing and spitting was getting to me too. I wondered if they took their wads out when they ate.

I slipped my car in gear. "Well, I appreciate your time."

"Hope our dogs didn't bother you none," he said. "Some folks're scared of 'em."

"Those cute puppies?" I said, and sped away.

FIFTEEN

I pulled into my parking space. Jamie had left traces of her perfume in the office. Oh, and lipstick smudges on the speaking end of the telephone receiver. She liked to work intimate when she was on the phone. I wiped off the worst of it and starting calling around for Bill Tomlin.

He wasn't at home, he wasn't at the small office Conners had kept in town, and he wasn't at the library where he spent most afternoons.

I did some work on legal cases and straightened the place up—someday I'd ask Jamie to help me, which should be a treat—and then I went back to calling around for Bill Tomlin.

Chris answered this time.

"Is Bill around?"

"We just got in. We were over at the funeral parlor with Dorothy. The wake's tomorrow night and that's when all the celebrities start coming. Hubert Humphrey and Jack Kennedy both said they'd be here."

"That's because the primaries are coming up."

"Oh, c'mon, McCain, you don't think Jack Kennedy's got any sort of chance against Hubert, do you?"

"You never know."

"The way he runs around? And he's not much of a thinker. Hubert and Richard went way back." Then: "I'll put Bill on."

Bill came on.

"You thirsty?"

"Just had a Pepsi, matter of fact."

"I was thinking of something a little stronger."

Hesitation. "What's going on, McCain?"

"We need to talk."

"About what?"

"A fishing cabin you visited from time to time."

Another hesitation. "You in real estate now?"

"This is getting awful cute. Meet me at the Home Run Club in half an hour."

WHAT I REALLY wanted to do was sit there and listen to Ray Charles. They had a couple of his songs on the jukebox. Just sit there sipping a 3.2 Hamm's draft, my head against the corner of the booth, my legs stretched out in front of me, just digging the music the way I had in high school, my head not stuffed with murder and red scares and zombies who sat solemn and silent in sunny back yards, the human debris of communist brain-washing. It was after work, and the motif was relief and relaxation. A lot of pure high prairie laughter, especially along the bar, where white collar drank with blue collar and nobody noticed.

He wasn't much bigger than I was, Bill Tomlin. He ordered a Falstaff and said, "You're smarter than I thought you were."

"Thanks."

"Of course, I had a pretty low opinion of you to begin with, so I'm not sure it's all that great a compliment."

"Fuck yourself, Tomlin. Fuck your education and fuck all your celebrity friends and fuck all your bullshit arrogance. I'm ready to throw this beer in your face and you give me half a reason to and I'll do it. You understand?"

"Wow. Counselor has a bad temper, doesn't he?"

A second later, beer was dripping from the shelf of his brow, from his nose, from his jaw. The booth was big enough that nobody had seen me splash him.

"You sonofabitch," he said.

"You're the only one left, Tomlin. Conners and Rivers and Cronin are dead. And the two girls sent out here aren't worth throwing a beer at. So you're elected."

He wiped himself off with a handkerchief. Beer had spilled onto his blue button-down shirt and tan sportcoat. I tossed him my handkerchief.

He said, "I should put this up your ass."

"Go ahead and try."

Two midgets talking tough. Norman Mailer would be proud of us.

He said, reluctantly using my handkerchief to finish the job, "I'm not your killer. And neither is Chris."

"No? You had a good reason. Conners was spending time with your wife; and Rivers and Cronin threatened to expose your meal ticket—namely, Conners. Power is what you're all after—power and that tape Conners made when Rivers and Cronin shot him up with Pentothal."

"He wasn't a communist."

"He sure had a lot of nice things to say about Joe Stalin."

"The right-wing press has vilified Stalin over here. He only did what he needed to do to hold his country together."

"To hold power. That's what you're really saying. And that's just what Joe McCarthy's defenders say, too. He was only doing what he needed to for the country."

"You must be a lonely man, McCain. A moderate with convictions." Contempt was clear in his voice. The only ones for him were the true believers.

I said, "Have you heard the tape?"

"How would I hear the tape?"

"Do you have any idea where it is?"

"None." He dabbed at his face.

I said, "You were in the garage Conners rented, approximately fifteen minutes before he was killed."

For the first time in our conversation, I'd succeeded in surprising him. It felt good. Too bad private eyes don't get gold stars for especially well-done jobs.

"How do you know that?"

I told him how I knew. And I also told him how I knew about his visits to the fishing cabin. By now he'd had time to recover. He no longer looked surprised, he looked angry.

"I should've let that bitch have it years ago.'

"Why didn't you?"

"Why do you think? Because I fucking love her, that's why. She's screwed half the men in town and I keep coming back for more. You have any idea how demeaning that is?"

"You just keep giving me more reason to think you killed Conners."

He sighed. He looked sad and old, startlingly so, and I was almost sorry I'd doused him with the beer. "I used to be fat." He raised his glass, but instead of taking a drink, he said, "The last several years with her—three or four pretty serious affairs, not to mention a lot of just general screwing—I've been seeing a psychiatrist. I can't eat, I can't sleep, I get these terrible migraines. And I stay with her."

"Maybe she killed him."

He shook his head. "No, they were alike. They both enjoyed sleeping around. She told me the sex was good."

At the risk of sounding like a rube, I said, "She told you that?"

"Sure. I asked her and she told me. We were having one of our arguments—this was the night Rivers was killed—and I asked her and she told me everything. I went crazy. I even started slapping her; I'm not proud of that. I might have done worse things if Dorothy hadn't gotten in late and heard Chris scream. She'd never seen me like that before—Dorothy, I mean. I think I scared her."

I looked at him. "I don't think I could handle it."

"I've left her twice already. She promises she'll change, and I come back. It's a little dance we do. Maybe I like it and I don't even know it."

"There're a lot of good women around to choose from."

He smiled coldly. "That why you wasted so much of your life on Pamela?"

"I was thinking the same thing."

"At least you're not smug. Nice girl like Mary and you treat her like shit. The whole town wonders about it."

"Maybe I'm changing."

"Pamela called, you'd go flying back. It could be your wedding day and you'd still go flying back. There're men who treat women the same way Chris and Pamela treat us. Neither sex has a monopoly on breaking hearts."

I said, "I'm sorry I threw that beer in your face."

He shrugged. "Somebody should've done it a long time ago. I tend to be insufferable. I don't have any balls, I just have poses. Richard said that to me once and I hated him for it."

I said, "I need to find the tape."

He nodded. "And what would you do with it?"

I hadn't thought about that before. "I'm not sure."

"If it reveals he was a communist, you'd destroy my meal ticket, as you called him. Nobody'd want a biography about a communist, not these days, they wouldn't. I have a big stake in that tape. It could cost me a lot of money. I probably have the biggest stake of all." He looked at his watch. "I wasn't planning on going back home. There's a concert in Iowa City tonight. Chamber music. Now I'll have to change. Chris wouldn't want to be seen with me looking this way. She's very particular about how her men look."

Neither of us made the effort to shake hands. I'm not sure why.

I STOPPED BY the office thinking to call Mary and see if she wanted to have dinner. Nice family-style restaurant that always served Swiss steak on mashed potatoes. Then a movie. There was a Robert Mitchum Western and a Doris Day romance at the second-run house. One for me; one for Mary. I kept thinking about what Bill Tomlin said—about spending your whole life at the mercy of somebody else. He'd managed to scare me. Mary wouldn't be hard to fall in love with at all.

The moment I reached for the doorknob, I heard a noise inside. I shouldn't bother to lock my door. People just let themselves in. The bus depot could lease space from me. We could put in a few chairs and lockers and maybe a hot dog stand.

The scent of the smoke was unmistakable: French. Gauloise. Judge Whitney.

She had made herself to home, as folks out here like to say. Parked her trim behind on the edge of my desk, one hand holding her French cigarette, the other a Peter Pan P-nut Butter glass filled with whiskey. My bottle of Jim Beam was open on the desk.

"This stuff," she pronounced, "is swill."

"Glad you're enjoying yourself. Most burglars are real nervous when they break into somebody's office."

"Hilarious as always, toots," she said. "Happen to see *The New York Times* this morning?"

"Afraid I didn't." She put her P-nut Butter glass down long enough to toss me the front section of the *Times*. "I thought it might interest you."

Not hard to find, what she was so irritated about. SMALL IOWA TOWN DEVASTATED BY "RED SCARE" MURDERS, OTHER STRIFE. I tossed it back on the desk.

"My guests have been having fun with me all day," she said, "and it's terrible. Fun at my expense is something I'm not used to. 'Oh, look, is that a commie over there behind that bush?' 'Oh, look, is that a commie submarine coming up out of the Iowa River?' They've even taken to making fun of Ayn Rand, which is really hard to take. Now, just when are you going to solve these damned murders and get this stuff off the front pages?"

"I'm doing what I can."

"Obviously it's not enough."

"How come you have all these liberal friends?"

"They play tennis and go yachting and spend half the year in Paris and London. They're fun to be around. So when I want fun, I go to them."

"What about conservatives?"

"Well, they have different things to do. Like count their money. Or complain that Dick Nixon is too liberal. They're just not quite so amusing." Then she said, "No word from our friend Pamela?"

"I'm not sure she's our friend. Not where I'm concerned, anyway."

"I told you long, long ago, McCain. Mary Travers is the one for you. You look cute together. Nice wholesome midwestern people. I'm afraid Pamela is a little out of your league. That's why you want her, of course. But that's exactly why you'll never have her."

"I think the subject's sort of moot," I said, "now that she's run off with Stu."

She sighed and took up Gauloise and whiskey once again. "God, I need some good brandy after the day I've had. I had to supervise all these trucks being unloaded."

I laughed. The prospect of Esme Anne Whitney being within three miles of a truck being unloaded struck me as hilarious. "You had to supervise what?"

"That damned charity I agreed to head up this year. I had to sit in this freezing warehouse while they unloaded the trucks. I had to tell them if their merchandise was something we wanted to offer at the sale next weekend. And then Dorothy Conners deliberately tried to scare me—pretended she didn't see me sitting there and damned near ran over me. She's a tough old broad. Communist women usually are. You should see her throw heavy things around."

The image came unbidden. *A panel truck with a body in it. Dragging the corpse of Rivers up my back stairs to hide it in my closet.* And then I thought of something else. "Excuse me a minute, Judge."

I called the motel where Rivers had been staying. Esther Haley, the woman I'd spoken with the other day, was on the desk. She had to think a minute before she answered my question. But then she said, "Now that you mention it, McCain, I think you're right. I think there was."

While I was talking, I could feel Judge Whitney watching me, and out of the corner of my eye I saw a puff of smoke hanging in the air.

After I hung up, I headed for the door.

"Where're you going?" the Judge called after me.

"I've got an errand to run."

"I hope it has something to do with this case."

"As a matter of fact," I said, as I reached the door, "it does."

Just as I got outside, I saw the black convertible. It was parked across the street and the blonde was in it, the blonde from a couple of years ago. A fantasy blonde—so cool, so fetching. Once she'd even sent me a photo of her sitting in the car. Who was she? What did she want? She pulled away. I wished I had time to hop in my own ragtop and follow her.

SIXTEEN

I took the road this time instead of the river. When I got a quarter mile from the Conners manor house, I put the car behind a copse of scrub pines—though not very close, the way the pines weep sticky stuff over everything below—and circled back around so I'd come out in the woods behind the house.

Even in brilliant moonlight, the woods were dark. You couldn't see the forest animals but you could hear them, leaping, crawling, scuttling, digging. The river smelled cold, the woods smelled tart, a scent I associate with autumn. I carried the shovel I keep in the trunk for emergencies, usually winter ones.

Lights burned everywhere in the house. They might have been having a party. I was self-conscious about crossing the back yard to the incinerator. I was even more so about dragging the bench of a redwood picnic table over to it.

I went to work. I spent 90 percent of my time digging and 10 percent glancing up at the windows on the three floors of the manor house. I didn't see anybody.

The incinerator was filled with ash of various weights and

textures. I rarely dug into anything solid. Not long before I was sweating. Not long before I was standing on my toes so I could shovel deeper in the five-foot-tall cylinder. I could feel the ash on my sticky face. My white shirt was grimy. Shamuses should get dry-cleaning discounts.

I went Eureka! two or three times for no good reason at all, the simple nudge of the shovel edge against anything solid filling me with hope.

But there was no reason for hope. I had found nothing useful, not until I was about three-quarters of the way down. By then I wasn't only on tippy-toes, I was damned near hanging over the edge. I knew instantly what it was. Which was when, of course, a silhouette appeared in a second floor window. I recognized the shape of her. I had to move.

But I didn't move fast enough. By the time I was jumping down from the bench, my find in my hand, she was bursting out the back door in her dark cardigan sweater, paint-splashed jeans, and a .38 special that she handled with alarming dexterity.

She knew what I'd found.

She didn't say anything and neither did I.

She was out of breath and the .38 was trembling a bit in her hand. She kept it pointed right at my heart.

Then she reached out and took it from me. Almost reluctantly. As if she didn't want to touch it.

"I didn't even listen to it, McCain, can you believe it?"

I said, "Sometimes it's better not to know the truth."

"He worked so hard all his life to do the right thing. And then he lets some stupid woman—she might well have been a Russian agent—talk him into helping her. Slipping her a few secrets here and there. He told me all about it one night when he was drunk."

She apparently didn't hear the back door open behind her. Or see the shadow slip silently across the stone patio.

"I couldn't have our name destroyed that way," Dorothy said. "There's no mark worse than treason. None. And of course it had to be a woman. None of them were any good. None of them."

"So you killed Rivers and Cronin?"

"They'd drugged him, and he'd told them the truth." She sounded weary now. "I had to have the tape. What choice did I have?"

"So none of us was good enough for your dear sweet son?"

Dorothy turned and saw Dana. Both women held handguns. I suddenly realized what had happened.

"You killed Richard, didn't you, Dana?" I said.

"Dear sweet Richard, you mean? Honest Richard? Faithful Richard?" I'd just begun to realize how drunk she was. "Three different times I caught your dear sweet son in bed with somebody else, Dorothy. And I'm sure he treated his other wives the same way."

Dorothy sounded astonished. "*You* killed him? You killed Richard?"

"I wish I could say I regretted it, but I don't. And I feel sorry for you that you don't understand. He was a totally selfish, arrogant man. You loved him too much. Much too much. You drove your own husband away because of how you loved your son."

"You killed him," Dorothy whispered, as if she couldn't comprehend the thought.

"She was trying on dresses in one of the back rooms at Fran's," I said. "She knew just about when he'd be pulling into the garage. She was right across the alley. Very slick."

Looking at the grotesque piece of melted plastic Dorothy held in her hand, Dana said, "God, what's that?"

"The tape Rivers and Cronin doped him up to get."

"The tape that would've destroyed the great Richard Conners."

"We'll never know," I said. "The only people who heard this tape are dead. Dorothy suspects what's on it, but that's a long way from knowing."

I stepped over to Dana, who wore a man's russet-colored crew neck sweater and jeans, and put my hand out. "I'd like the gun."

"It's not even loaded."

"I'd still like it."

She said, "I'm sorry, Dorothy. The funny thing is, I've always liked you. You have a good heart and a good mind and you're very, very brave. There aren't many women around like that. Or men, for that matter. I'm not sorry for Richard. But I *am* sorry for you."

I took the gun from her hand and turned toward Dorothy, which was when Dana took a few steps toward us. "Please forgive me, Dorothy."

My sense was that she was going to embrace the older woman. She was drunk now and sounding forlorn. Her arms reached out.

And that's when Dorothy shot her: twice, in the chest.

I can't tell you what happened in the next minute or so. Something happened to my voice. I made some kind of animal noise I'd never heard before. And then I was kneeling next to Dana. There was blood. My own sobs. Her arms and legs were spasming. I'd never seen anything uglier or more terrifying, the way this woman was dying. I leaned over and kissed her on the forehead, a desperate good-bye kiss.

From somewhere I heard a barn owl cry and saw the moonlight make Dana's classic face oddly lovely in its horror, the light almost mythic in this relinquishing of life.

At some time I heard the noise of another bullet being fired. No cry this time, just a moan, and I barely had time to turn to see her fall, already dead, the bullet to the temple so swift, to lie upon the land she'd loved so much.

Sometime, somehow, I stumbled into the house and called Cliffie and poured myself a drink. There was nothing to do about the two women now, nothing at all.

SEVENTEEN

By eleven o'clock, I was tired of all the calls. You know, people congratulating me on figuring the whole thing out. Mom and Dad, Sis from Chicago ("Don't tell the folks, but I'm dating this man who's ten years older than I am," which depressed the hell out of me but I was too tired to argue), some reporters wanting interviews, Natalie and arch-enemy drinking-buddy Margo both getting gassed at a neat place called the Airliner in Iowa City, two people I'd gone to high school with but hadn't talked to for a long time ("Remember the night you got bombed, McCain, and stood up on top of the memorial cannon in the city park and took a leak?" and other such hallowed memories), and finally Mary.

"Gee," I said. "I've been trying to get you all night."

"Sorry. I was—out, I guess."

"You guess?"

Something was wrong.

"How'd you like the blouse?"

"Oh, the blouse." She'd forgotten. "I'm sorry. It's—beautiful, McCain. It really is. But I can't accept it."

"Why not?"

Long pause. "This afternoon."

"Yes. This afternoon?"

"Wes came up and took my apron off me and said, 'We're going for a drive.' Just like that."

"And you went for a drive."

"And we talked."

"About?"

"Personal stuff."

"And?"

"And McCain, he started crying. Just sobbing. I've never seen him like that. I mean, I've seen him cry but I've never seen him so—humble. He said he was sorry for all the mean things he's ever said to me and he wants us to get married right away. Just do it. Don't wait for a big church wedding or anything."

The way things were going, I was going to be the one who was sobbing.

"McCain?"

"Yeah?"

"Why don't you say something?"

"Because I don't know what to say."

"I just never realized before how much he loves me. I need to think things over."

I sighed. "Yeah, I suppose that's how it's got to be."

"It's kinda funny, isn't it? For the first time it looked like we—you and I—would get together, and then Wes comes along and—"

"I think I'll go now."

"You really should take the blouse back."

"Just bring it to work and I'll pick it up."

"It's all kinda crazy, isn't it?"

"Yeah," I said. "I guess that's a good way to describe it."

* * *

I WAS SCARED and I prayed. The old Our Fathers and the old Hail Marys. I was scared and confused; I felt like I was eight in terms of wisdom and eighty-eight in terms of spirit. *I wish I was an old man and love was through with me.* Somebody wrote that once and I've never forgotten it, but I couldn't tell you who it was.

Thoughts like that here in the Lucky Strike–Hamm's beer darkness. TV on but no sound. Me propped up in bed. The three cats fanned out all around me. A little Miles Davis on the turntable.

I thought of all the dead people too. And all the red scare bullshit and how I hated both sides. And Dorothy. Eyes so forlorn in death, tears collected in the corners of their sockets.

I stubbed my cigarette out and went to sleep, clothes and all. Needing to pee. Not caring if I ever woke up again.

And then sometime somewhere the phone rang and I groped for it, badly disoriented, wondering who the hell would call this late, and then I got scared thinking maybe something had happened to somebody in my family.

But when I got the receiver to my ear, a voice I didn't recognize at first said, "McCain. Listen. I have to whisper. Or he'll hear me."

"Who is this?"

"It's Pamela, you dope. We have this big hotel suite. He's in the bathroom right now. Oh, McCain. I've made a terrible, terrible mistake. I'm going to sneak out of here tomorrow and take the train back to Iowa City. Can you meet me at the depot at seven P.M.? Then, frantic: "Oh, God, here he comes!"

And she hung up.

I lay there and lit another Lucky and thought of another great line. This one I knew the source of: E. M. Forster: *Beauty makes its own rules.*

It sure as hell does, I thought. It sure as hell does.